A SONG FOR CARMINE

M Spio

AuthorHouse™ LLC
1663 Liberty Drive
Bloomington, IN 47403
www.authorhouse.com
Phone: 1-800-839-8640

Published by AuthorHouse   03/29/2014

ISBN: 978-1-4918-9985-4 (sc)
ISBN: 978-1-4918-9984-7 (hc)
ISBN: 978-1-4918-9983-0 (e)

Library of Congress Control Number: 2014905604

Prince Edward's Court
www.one2one.com
(877) 407-9797

PROLOGUE

THE FIRST COLORED BOY I ever saw was a dead one, left to die in an old warehouse on the edge of town. I have never been able to forget his face, the layer of dust on his skin, the way his tears left clear streaks down his face, his fists in knots. Sometimes I walk the streets of that old neighborhood with my son, especially when fall is coming and the leaves are beginning to change and the air has a chill to it. There's no way not to remember—I do—but I know enough now to know there's no use fighting it.

Still, I don't know how this white boy ended up raising a black son. In so many ways, life is all a mystery to me.

They was just fixin' to scare him, they said, have a little fun; it wasn't supposed to end up that way. That's what the papers said anyway.

The night had been real inky and wet. Downtown Eton is all blinking stoplights and dark store windows, and in the distance, the ridges of the Appalachians glow, the tips of them a faded deep blue.

It had just gone too far. I was just a kid, but I knew that. I'd seen too many things cross that line, the one between bad and worse. At some point, these things start carrying themselves, get a mind of their own, a current so strong you can't stop it.

*　*　*

We pass around a forty-ounce beer; it is warm and sour in my mouth and I don't like it much, but we keep on drinking because it's the thing to do. There's an old man that hangs around the corner store on Fifth Street, and if we buy him a pack of smokes, he gets us anything we want.

Our bikes lean up against the curb, stacked on each other, the streetlights bouncing off their frames, the mosquitoes following us. Our shirts stick to our bodies; it is the hottest point of the summer, mid-August, the air heavy and thick. We'll be starting high school soon.

I use the bottom of my T-shirt to wipe my brow and shift my weight on the sidewalk, see the strings of my shoes beneath my feet, notice the full moon in the sky, look around at my friends. Life has started doing this lately. Stopping, I mean. Sometimes it seems like I can get a real good look at it.

I think about a lot of things lately. Seems like lately that's all I do. I want to grow up and get out of here because everything ends up bad around here. It's true. Things don't make a lot of sense. The right things don't lead to the right other things, and I don't understand. I'm supposed to believe in God—after all, my pa is a damn preacher. God hasn't ever stopped anything from happening, never intervened where he should've, never saved anybody. Not that I've seen, anyway.

Sometimes we ride our bikes on the trails in the woods surrounding Eton, all the way to the edge of town, and we talk about leaving. Running away together. Seeing what else is out there. We look down at the beaten red clay road leading out of town each time, sit, then turn around and start pedaling back in.

To what, I don't know. It's just that the big world is still scary, I guess. But me, I will leave, I know I will. I have to. This place is eating me alive.

Ma and Pa are still checked out most of the time, drunk just after the sun's gone down or caught up on pieces of scripture they can't seem to understand. They force it down my throat, make me chew on things I can't swallow. Seems like all Ma does is ignore me, and Pa hits me. I try to get by.

I walk over to my bike and climb on. It's too early and too hot to stay this still. "Let's get out of here," I say, and we follow the bumpy road along the railroad tracks. I weave in and out of the streets, up and down hills, over the familiar terrain and far away from the street I live on. Mark and Griff follow. We've been together our whole lives almost. I like having them around, seeing them most days, knowing we got stuff in common.

We end up near the old railroad crossing, the one that crosses Magnolia Street, the familiar light blinking red, the sound of metal hitting metal still hovering in the trees. There's a certain symmetry, a rhythm to it all. I like knowing that.

Some nights we come here and sit and wait for the train to pass, getting high off the rusty pitch of the sound so close to our ears, the feel of the rushing wind skirting our faces, watching the empty cars come sliding past and thinking about how characters in movies jump right on, how the train don't think about anything, how it just keeps on keeping on.

Sometimes when we're at the creek throwing rocks or in Mark's living room playing video games, we start talking about it—how we could jump on that train, get away from our fathers, this dusty old town, these woods. Maybe join the circus or ride until we come to one of those little mining towns in Virginia. We'll disappear; we could be the men our families say we'll never be.

We look down each way to see if the train is coming, if we can hear the old whistle blow in with the wind, see the eye of the light, or feel the heavy vibrations under our feet. We wait.

The smell of pine is strong, deep, and green, the leaves move with the wind, and it's a sound like fabric pushing up against a lady's legs. Otherwise, the night is so still. So big and still. There is nothing but a deep void in it. We're always looking for ways to fill it, seems like.

We get off our bikes and sit on the tracks, a sky full of stars above us. We don't talk about anything, but we share just the same. Ma says it won't always be like it's been, that Jesus's gonna make it right, but I don't know. Mark and Griff talk about their folks, what goes on behind their closed doors, and I feel for them, only they don't have preachers as their old men and they can be regular mess-ups.

We sit on the curb and pass the forty around again. Every once in a while a car passes, slows down when it gets close to us, before speeding off again. Everyone knows everyone around here, and it's not easy keeping any secrets.

We laugh, throw rocks over the tracks, finish the beer before throwing the glass bottle into the woods. It makes a rustling sound as it falls through branches and leaves, and then makes a dull thud on the ground.

We all seem to be lost in our own thoughts until we hear noises coming from the old warehouse across the street. Its walls are paper-thin, rusty, and red, and we can see light bouncing around inside. We hear voices, laughter, a few bottles being kicked across the ground, glass rolling over gravel, clinking. Next to the warehouse, there are rows of old houses, pinks, blues, dogs chained up in the yards, old cars up on blocks. On this side of town, you can bring anything, do anything; almost everything over here has already been done.

"What was that, man?" Griff asks. We hear someone pleading in a raspy, bated voice.

"Probably some kids playin' around." Mark nudges forward, listens closer. We hear people in that old building all of the time. Sometimes we get up the nerve to go over there and investigate, and usually it's a homeless person, sometimes kids we know in there smoking weed, or a prostitute passing through.

We get back on our bikes, look for the train again, chew on pieces of wheatgrass, roll back and forth on the gravel. I can feel the humidity pressing my hair to my forehead. I shake my head.

Across the street the voices get louder, taunting, jabbing. We hear the long, piercing words, the syllables that stretch out when someone is being hurt with words. Yooooouuuuuu. Weeeee . . . Whaaaaaat. Whhhhyyyyy.

"You got nowhere to go," I hear someone say. "Just try to run. What are you doing here anyway?" There's more noise. The warehouse vibrates louder with voices, and in the distance, I finally hear the old train whistle, count the seconds until I know it will pass us. I feel satisfied for a brief second.

I get off my bike and walk close to the tracks. I like to stand on the metal when the train is approaching, feel the melodic vibrations deep in my body, stand there until the very last second, until the guys are yelling at me to get off and to quit goofing off, until we're all afraid of what I'll do.

The train is getting closer. I can feel it hum beneath my feet and I get excited. In the distance, the katydids chirp. I feel the wind push the trees around. Everything seems to happen all at once, but separate too.

I look away from the light of the train when I see a group of kids running out of the warehouse, a blur of colored T-shirts. They're older and bigger than us, their legs longer, voices deeper. I hear broken bottles clink on the gravel and feet hitting the rocks fast. They're chasing someone, a dark, lone figure several yards in front of them. One of them picks up a bottle and runs faster.

I think time stops for a minute, but I don't know for sure. I've seen a lot happen in my time, and I know that somewhere babies are being born and people are saying prayers, and somewhere else women are being raped and elderly are rotting in beds and God is turning the other cheek. I'm just trying to put it all together.

*   *   *

I hear them back inside the warehouse. There's no light inside now, but the moon's above us and the three of us are so quiet. I hear Ma in my head.

I look back to see if I can see the train's eye yet, remember what Ma said earlier that morning.

"You know, Carmine, it ain't that bad. Life ain't supposed to be a bed of roses, you know. Stuff happens." She takes a long drag from her menthol and I stare at her face, look deep into her eyes—we share the same blue. I breathe in her cloud of smoke and say okay.

"I know things ain't always so great, but they're gonna get better, Carmine. You'll see." She stubs her cigarette out and starts washing a pan in the sink. I head out the back door.

I hear someone scream back inside the warehouse. It's more like a howl, a long sorrowful sound. I don't know how to place it. Mark and Griff push their bikes closer to the street.

I look across the street and see people running out of the building. I look away and up at the sky. There are a million stars in it; some of them seem to float. It's times like these that I want to leave my body, float away somewhere, be something that sits in a place, does just the one thing, can't be hurt by any of this down here.

*   *   *

We walk over, creep around, trip over pieces of metal on the ground, old pieces of railroad track, smell the mildew, the old wood holding it together. The building seems strange all of a sudden, as though I've never been in it, never kicked cans around the ground, never spent a night here hiding from Pa.

I find him first. I think I hear the wheezing sound of something rubbing together; turns out it's him trying to breathe. I can smell the blood. It is acidic and wet. The wind blows through the building and whistles, a lone sound. There is nothing else to be heard out there.

I knew he was nearly dead. There was just too much pouring out of him, seeping, really, already torn to pieces. His skin, so dark, dark as coal, still glows in the light of passing cars. I look at him so closely, only a sliver of the whites of his eyes showing, an afterthought really.

I feel a strange mixture of disgust, repulsion, then sympathy. Is he an animal or someone like me? I remember when Pa used to take me to Klan meetings, so deep in the woods, no one could see the flames of the bonfires shooting up at the sky, hear the chants, a garble of words I could never understand. I sat on Pa's shoulders and tried to make sense of it all: the bitter hate, the closed white sheets, the secrets.

I look down again at the boy, feel the urge to kick him, roll him over, something. I don't know what I'm supposed to do.

"Is he dead, you think?" Griff walks to the edge of the building and then back, looking for someone, I think, someone other than us.

"I don't know. I don't know." I turn and look at Mark; he's sitting on the ground holding his knees.

"It's not our fault, you know?" I say.

He nods, but doesn't move.

The sight of life leaving the world spirals, twists, like water slowly turning down a drain or all eight of a bug's legs flailing in unison. There's an energy, a symmetry to it, a certain beauty. You feel like it's not that much different from life, but something similar, one thing leading to something like the next.

"I think he's dead now," I say quietly. I lean down to him, close to his chest, feel revolted and afraid and empty all at the same time. I hear nothing move but the crickets outside, the rumble of the approaching train. It is nearly upon us now; it'll be here and gone in a second.

"He probably ain't dead; he's probably faking it." Griff walks closer, starts to laugh a little and then stops. He pulls a pack of cigarettes out of his back pocket and lights one up.

"I don't know . . . Did you hear him scream? Did you hear all those bottles break?" Mark is shaking, looking around, stares at me for a second and then looks away.

I sit on the ground beside the boy. The train passes, its light shining in the building. I see his bloody shirt, the big gash in his head now, the way his legs are twisted up beneath his body. I see the sliver of his brown eyes; they stare off into a space I do not know, but they twitch at the edges, and I jump up.

I think I see his head move so slightly, could've been the light, probably was the light, because the blood still pours out warm from the gash in his head and pools beside him.

I consider what my Pa'd do in this moment, remember the burning crosses, the division in our little town, whites on one side, blacks the other. Don't know where I fit in, but know I got no reason to do anything about what I've seen done.

I sit for a minute longer, feel the rumble until I know it's gone, run out of the building, and try to catch the last of that light.

"Let's get out of here. Somebody'll find him—eventually." I put my head down as I say it, shuffle out of the warehouse. The sky is a dark gray, wet and hollow. I can hear the train somewhere in the distance. I shake my head and start to cry. Life is worse than I thought.

CHAPTER I

I HAVE A TALL bottle of Jim Beam in my hand. I hold its narrow neck and tip it back into my mouth. The sour liquid rolls down my throat easily, hardly a burn to it. I am slurring and singing old church hymns, centered on the ledge of the window fourteen stories up, with my back against the windowsill, one bare leg hanging out of it. I have lived on the edge my whole life; this is nothing new.

The wind is whistling almost in jest, my eyes blurring with the city lights below me. I sing louder. "Since I laid my burden down . . ." I laugh, remember the lines in Mississippi John Hurt's face, know it ain't quite the same for me, but that I got a song too.

My mouth dries and my eyes begin to water. I swing my legs back and forth over the ledge, dare the weight of my bitter self to pull me down. I look out on the city of Dallas, search it, feel like a king, then a pauper, don't want to be anything if I can't be the man I've been so far.

I think about God, still wonder if he exists at all, remember Pa's church. The building, triangular at the top, its white siding, like Pa himself, so fragile, always at the mercy of the changing wind. What power does anyone really have?

I remember the feeling of uncooked rice beneath my knees as Pa punished me for something and told me to pray for forgiveness, to ask to be good, to show some goddamn respect. I wanted to be good. I remember the way his face looked as I stared at him, hovering above me, the coarse whiskers on this face, beat yellow by the sun, the smell of Ma's chicken grease in the air, all the little details stick out.

I haven't thought of Eton, Georgia (population 319), in years, but the memory of my father haunts me tonight. As if he'd always expected everything to end up this way for me, the prodigal son, personal failure the only thing possible for me. I bet he's somewhere laughing right about now, kicked back in a chair, whiskey in one hand, tattered Bible in the other.

I left Eton after high school and hit the ground running, running as fast as I could, out west, to another life, from the kid I'd been. Somehow I managed to navigate my way into a scholarship at Southern Methodist University in Dallas, and the rest is history.

I wanted a better place to self-destruct, to live out my escape, anyplace other than Eton—no, I wanted a place that could swallow Eton whole and spit it out, a place where I could disappear. At SMU, I became unidentifiable among the other slugs there: I was popular, loud, drunk most of the time. I made an art out of handling straight shots of bourbon, holding back mouthfuls of digested pizza. For breakfast, I would gulp down hard liquor and fill my mouth full of chewing tobacco. After graduation, the advertising world welcomed me with daily libations. A martini here, a screwdriver there, and then you were among friends.

Advertising—it's the ultimate poison. Find out what people like, what makes them feel good, figure out a way to feed them the illusion of it, make them think they can actually have it.

Car commercials—leather seats, cruise control, wide tires, open highways, surround sound—I could put it all together and make someone feel like they'd never be alone, never have to hurt if they'd just buy that car, use that cream, subscribe to that idea, believe in those glossy words.

Credit cards were keys to real futures, soft and forgiving, forever young and safe. Even laundry soap could change a whole life. I knew what people wanted—deep down, I wanted the same things—but it was all smoke and mirrors.

Sometimes late at night, after I'd gotten laid by some girl I'd picked up at a bar, I'd pull out my old tapes, catalogs, pray to the manipulating copy, laugh out loud to the glossy commercials, write notes as I paced the room and thought of other ways to market happiness and safety and true love. It was power.

Melanie finds me out there on that ledge, humming to myself, punching right hooks into the air. She's been in and out of my life for years. There are pieces of a shattered champagne bottle everywhere on the terrazzo floors in my apartment, soaked drafts of presentations for the Carmichael account, an Armani suit, tie, Kenneth Cole shoes, other parts of my costume. She steps carefully through the rummage, careful not to step on the broken glass, and looks at me the way she always has. She longs. I falter. Together we are the things we both hate.

She startles me and the whiskey bottle falls out of my hand and down thirteen floors. The sound of the glass breaking, the implications of everything I do, so far away in the distance I can barely hear.

It all came crashing down. I'd forgotten it was actually possible to lose. The Carmichael account—it was ubiquitous. I'd come so far; I was to be a partner in the firm. It was supposed to be the top of a ladder I'd spent years climbing without looking down, a life of Superdome dreams, vodka martinis and sky-rise apartments. The last few years of my life have been a blur. My career became my religion, my identity, and the Carmichael account was to secure my spot in that superficial heaven.

I remember getting the news—the initial sense of relief that came, quick like lightning, then the anger. It happened so fast.

No one saw it coming, or maybe we did. It's one of those things that you wonder why you let happen—a $25 parking ticket that you don't pay till it becomes $600, a dull ache in your side that explodes into appendicitis, the small thread of your sweater that you let unwind until there's only a ball of yarn and nothing left.

Diego, the head honcho, called a meeting. It was quick and painless. The ride was over. No door prizes, no "you were here" T-shirt, nothing. The Carmichael account was gone, and there was nothing left for any of us.

I'd known Diego for years—heard all the stories about how he'd started out mopping these floors for a living, how he now owned them. He was a powerhouse. He hired me just out of college, and I wanted to be him. I wanted his life. The top floor, the women, the money, the power. He was everything Pa wasn't. He believed in himself; he had the power to conquer life, manipulate it, sculpt it into whatever he wanted it to be. To me, he was what a man was supposed to be.

I became his shadow, his protégé, and he taught me everything. He taught me how to pick up women and write copy and tailor my suits and schmooze clients, hold my drink, and draft airtight contracts. I was the son he'd never had, but secretly I planned to take him down, to wipe these floors with him someday, to be him, but better.

Sometimes I would find him in his office very late at night as I wandered the halls punching right hooks into the air, considering the exit sign, and thinking of new ways to climb and conquer and run away from anything just under the surface. I didn't want to go home, but I didn't really know what else I could do there either. Diego always sat quietly, his head in his hands, breathing so softly, the dim light of his desk lamp putting shadows on the walls, his face. There was more to the story. A man is rarely just the one thing.

He was always there. He created Icarus Media, worked his whole life for it and only it, and it was all he had. Sometimes I'd study the deep, brown lines in his face, notice how the skin of his cheeks sagged, how he frowned from someplace deep. He'd spent his whole life climbing and walking on people and not looking back. The point was not lost on me completely.

After the announcement from Diego, I found an empty box, walked into my office, remembered a bottle of gin in the back of my drawer, tipped it back, and then proceeded to tear up everything. Without the Carmichael account, none of it meant anything. Not a goddamn thing. I didn't want to end up like Diego, but I didn't want this either.

I walked out, empty box in hand, gin bottle in the other. I got into my BMW, turned the music up really loud, and sucked down the dry gin as I drove a hundred miles an hour down the interstate, daring death to come take me. I wanted an easy out.

*   *   *

When Melanie finds me on the ledge, I've already been there for hours, laughing at the irony of it all, the way the mythical Icarus (Diego's hero) had gotten too close to the sun and burned his wax wings.

"What are you doing here?" She knows trouble and she seeks it and leaves its wake behind her. We go way back, this woman and I, and I can remember the path and its bumps, but I don't want to anymore.

She's dressed in a tight black dress which covers the voluptuous curves of a woman meant for prostitution or martyrdom; a girl who's childhood dreams included self-inflicted wounds and chases that never ended, nightmares in ranch-style homes whose shade of brown never pales with age. But like many women, her station in life is necessary and appropriate and it keeps her all but happy.

Melanie's blonde hair has the acidity of a mixed drink, wicked and potent. She looks happy in my bed, in a glass of ice, vacant but fitting, cold but kind.

I watch her as she picks pieces of glass up off the floor. She's beautiful—hollow, but beautiful.

"Picking up the pieces, as usual," she tells me.

"I've lost it all, you know," I tell her as I tip the bottle back again. I lean my head back and tap it on the cement wall; the traffic glows below me. It would only take one small move.

"What did you have to lose?" She walks to the kitchen and grabs another bottle of whiskey, takes a long, hard drink before handing it to me.

"Good question," I tell her.

I pull myself off the ledge and walk into the kitchen. When I turn the light on, I get a good look at Melanie, run my eyes over the contours of her red lips, notice the threads in her skintight dress, try to feel anything that resembles love.

I'd fucked women by the handful for years. Melanie just hung around, a glutton for punishment. I sampled them like shiny bottles behind a bar, the women tall and slender and light, sometimes cold to the touch, but always willing, long hair and light eyes, just out of college, middle-aged, it was all the same. The women were always as willing as the bottle, and I got off on it, the getting and the taking and the leaving. I consumed them.

"Hey, baby . . ." I could turn on the southern charm when it was needed. I kept it in my pocket like the smallest of pills I could whip out on the fly. It slid down their throats like water, made them give me keys to apartments I would never visit more than once. I'd seen Pa work people the same way.

I saw only figures, shapes, and curves—shadows really. I never saw eyes or heard real voices. I wasn't that discerning. Bartenders were fair game, easy, within reach. They were cheap and disposable, easy to find. In some way they expected it. I regarded them less than the secretaries at the firm, whose stares would pierce my back as I walked by their desks.

I never met a match; they came and they went. Occasionally I thought of my mother. If I awoke in the night, in the early morning hours, sometimes I would find her sitting quietly in one corner of my mind, fidgeting, looking for me. Melanie was the only woman I ever really got to know, but only very distantly.

I open the fridge and pull out a wedge of cheese, a jar of pickles; under the cabinet there are crackers. I grab two glasses and pour them half full of whiskey.

I go to my bedroom to find a clean T-shirt, and when I come back, she's set the table for us. Sometimes it's like this. Our defenses low, we become just two people.

She's followed me for years like a stray puppy, and I've never considered it much. I take a good look at her across the table, wonder what she thinks of me now that it's all over, that I've got no temple to stand upon.

"Melanie, I've cared for you . . ." My eyes dart all over the kitchen, away from her eyes. I pick up a piece of cheese and a cracker and put them both in my mouth.

She laughs, pushes her glass into mine so that they clink loudly.

"Carmine, don't bother. None of it matters anyway." She stands up and walks past me into the bedroom.

She's in my bedroom searching for her belongings. The glue that has held the remainders of this relationship together over the years: a pair of earrings she's hidden away in my nightstand drawer, a toothbrush behind the old can of shaving cream in the medicine cabinet, a small T-shirt at the back of my bottom drawer.

She says, "I feel so ridiculous for always coming around like this. You never gave me anything, and now you have nothing to give."

I remember the Valentine's Day several years ago when she'd given me flowers and a card that said, "You were made to love me, so why don't you?" I'd laughed out loud in the moment, pushed the card across my desk. I turn my eyes inside, squint when I remember how I'd promised to take her to dinner that night but had driven to a nearby lake and fished naked all night.

"I feel like a fool, Carmine, for loving you at all, because you don't know how to love anyone." She walks into the bathroom and slams the door behind her.

"Mel, please come out of there. I'll try to change. You'll see." I think of the prospect of having no job, no woman, nothing to fill all the space life contains.

I open the bathroom door and look right at her, kneel down to her and start to unbutton her dress, push my face into hers. Without looking her in the face, I slide into her and begin thrusting, her sitting on the edge of the toilet, clawing at me. When we're done, I walk out of the room, close the door behind me, search the apartment for the whiskey bottle, and wait.

She comes out and stands in front of me. Her lipstick is smeared and her face is red. I lift up her leg and pull off her high-heeled red shoes, one at a time.

"What are you going to do?" Melanie asks. "What's next for you?" She looks at me longingly, as though I hold the answers for us both.

"What else is there?" I ask and tip the bottle back again. I start singing another hymn I remember from way back when, about how troubles come and troubles go and when I hear the phone ring, I am not completely surprised to hear Ma's voice on the machine, shaky and wet.

"Carmine—you need to come home, son. Your old man is dying."

I hear groans in the background, then Pa. "Is that my boy? Captain, captain . . ."

CHAPTER 2

THE OLD WIDE GREYHOUND bus whizzes past trees, meadows, dairy farms, patchwork quilts of fields—everything so stationary yet fleeting at the same time. The landscape changes from flat to hilly, then to mountainous and dark, the flatlands becoming hills, then inclines, then descents. My head pounds. I can still feel the whiskey traveling my veins, a muddy current.

When the light casts a reflection of myself onto the window each time it comes out of the shadows, I really get a good look at myself. I look like I've lived more than just thirty-two years. I can see the lines darting from the edges of my eyes, the slight sagging in my neck, the heavy fatigue. I've lived hard, but I've got nothing to show for it.

It gets harder and harder to keep my eyes open as the miles pass, the sun drowsing me, the bus rocking. I shift in my seat and watch the mile markers like they are birthdays, twenty-five, sixteen, twelve, five, remembering my life as they go, the things that have brought me here. I remember myself at five, a soft little boy, brown hair growing in pointed tendrils over my ears, my eyes bright. I am so small. The tenderness makes me wince, but the memory won't stop bleeding through.

I am on my father's shoulders and I can see part of his face, the sagging tan skin, the sharp whiskers; his hair is turning white at the edges and near his ears. I feel his body move us with each step, each of his feet landing with a heavy thump. We are both chanting something, some kind of game, both of us laughing and singing as we march through the woods surrounding Eton. He points out the names of trees, the sounds of different birds; the sun peaks through the tops of the trees and rests on our heads. When I look behind me, Ma is following, carrying a set of fishing poles and watching us. She is smiling too, full of energy, color in her cheeks.

Then it shifts.

I am nine years old, and the small church is filled to its small walls. The pews sag with parishioners, and the wet morning air speaks of the underside of life; there's an energy in the air, in my small body. I am still squeezed tight from the night before. I toy with a small red yo-yo, rolling it back and forth in my sweaty palm, look around the room, and then down at the floor. Ma sits next to me. She seems beaten and weathered, her body emanating a draft of scotch and sweat. I don't understand.

Pa is at the pulpit, his voice echoing through the drywall and arched ceiling, the cloth of his robe starched and clean, like an animal's coat; he is primed and ready for the fight.

"My brothers and my sisters, let me connect with you for a moment on this fine Sunday morning . . ." His voice trails off, and I can hear the Georgia come and go from his voice, the old Texas accent buried somewhere beneath it. I can't take my eyes off him; it's all I know, the thing that I want to really understand. I watch his arms rise and fall with his words, and he is God himself. I hold my breath and wait.

I am jerked back to the present when the bus comes to a hard stop and someone gets off. The landscape is starting to look familiar, so different from my neighborhood of skyscrapers in Dallas. I know these tall pine trees, recognize the twists and turns of these Georgia roads, how they disappear into the forest and then reemerge. The edges of the trees are beginning to change with the season, and the aspens look like they're holding bags of golden coins, the maples orange at their ends, the sky a sullen shade of blue. The mountains appear out of nowhere.

"Excuse me. I gotta get out; my stop's coming." I look at the man beside me, but only briefly. He's holding a crossword book and pen close to his face, and when he looks up at me, I can see the cataracts stretching over the glass of his eyes, wet in the corners. I have to look away.

I make my way to the front of the bus and feel everyone's eyes on me. I'm wearing old worn-out jeans, a military jacket, my black Adidas duffel bag, Lugz boots. I look at each of their faces, see the Georgia all over it: small eyes and pinched mouths, hair dull shades of yellows and browns, smiles that creep up their faces, words that come out sideways.

When the bus finally comes to a complete stop, I step off and look around. It's nearly eight in the evening, but there's almost nothing going on around me at the bus stop in downtown Eton. The buildings are so low to the ground, so much open sky, there is nothing covering anything.

I can hear a flag ding against its pole in the distance. A block away, a yellow light blinks above an empty intersection. When the wind blows, I hear the yelp of a tired dog, his howl searching for relief.

I stand at the bus stop and wait. I don't know what to do now. I remember the night before, how one cataclysmic event leads so easily to another, how they all pile up on top of each other, and you've got to figure out how to make it all stand.

*　　*　　*

A couple of hours later, I am in a red truck with my friends, buddies I used to call them. Griffin drives. I watch him peripherally. He looks pretty much the same as he did back then, a large-nosed, clean-cut guy with glasses. He's built like a quarterback, bulky and square; he lives within those lines. He's recently divorced and spends his nights at the bowling alley, at least that's what he tells me.

I ride shotgun. Mark sits in the backseat. He looks smaller than I remember, still short, stout, and a little quiet. He's got a family of three now and works at the chemical factory outside of town. Next to him, Jim, a guy I knew in school, sits. He has a roll of fat around his middle and spits when he talks.

We drive around on the dark back roads that twist in and out of the old mountains and drink beer. I haven't seen or talked to any of them since I left, but when the night air rushes in and out of the car, I can't help but remember that inky night by the train tracks. We never talked about it.

"I've got just the thing to keep your mind off things, brother. It's good you're back." Griff looks at me out of the corner of his eye as he talks, and it feels good to be something simple for a while.

"All I need is a good bottle of something," I say as I down the last beer. "This beer ain't gonna cut it. I prefer scotch these days, something with a strong wicked taste."

"That's easy; we'll get you more than that . . . doctor's orders," Griff says as he takes a sharp turn with the bend of the road, the engine picking up momentum and then lagging with a dull roar.

"The pet doctor's orders," Mark laughs from the backseat.

We drive past a billboard with a black politician. He's tall, with broad shoulders, his eyes warm behind his glasses

"Was that Dwayne Johnson?" I ask.

"Yeah—he's running for sheriff or some shit." Jim flicks a cigarette out the window and messes with the knob on the radio.

"Eton sure has changed." I remember us again, that summer night, the last fourteen years of bravado, the twitch in my legs. I laugh to myself.

"No, not really. The niggers just got bolder." Griff takes a long drink from his can of beer and laughs.

I watch the gray pavement twist in and out of the hills, the tall narrow trees shaking loose, the car's headlights barely enough to light the dark way.

"I can't believe I'm back here, I really can't." I say it smugly. "This place still has nothing for me."

We pick up a bottle of whiskey at the corner liquor store and talk about old times, the windy roads pushing up into the hills, then back again, the sky growing so black. We drive until we hit the end of roads, till there is nothing but forest in front of us. I tell them about my two-thousand-dollar suits, how beautiful the big-city women are, how good they smell (and taste). I tell them about the empire I'm about to build on my own because the other one wasn't good enough. My voice carries, and I sing it to them.

"Carmine, dude, people don't really change." Griff takes a sharp left and heads up yet another hill, Eton is all slopes and descents; we've never done anything but go up and down them.

"You ain't any different than you were." He laughs and looks at me for a second before looking at the road again.

"That's where you're wrong, my friend." I study the road ahead of me and think of all the ways I'll show them.

*   *   *

The town has not changed. There's a corner store, an old trading post selling antiques, a diner, a gas station with a couple of teenagers lingering around it, one road in and one road out, a post office, the sheriff's station, no one on the streets, the shells of houses glowing light in the dark.

I feel nausea, anxiety. My insides churn, and I want to get out of there, feel the buzz of Dallas, hear the car horns and the sounds of planes above, feel the money, live in the cocoon. I can't stand this.

"You can do this, Carmine," I tell myself. I still feel the hum of the whiskey on my insides, the slow burn of my liver, the blackness of sweet escape, the goofy laughs of my old friends, the sting of Griff's words.

I look at the houses in my old neighborhood, small houses with big green yards and Confederate flags hanging in the front, old rocking chairs on porches, fake flowers in flower boxes. Can any of this actually be real?

The sky is so dark above me, the streetlights barely glow; I haven't known darkness like this in so long. The air is so quiet, no cars rushing past, no voices hanging out of buildings. There is no pulse, nothing alive here. I feel a wave of panic wash over me.

I walk a few blocks from where my friends have dropped me off, get lost in the sound of my feet hitting the old pavement. When I look up again, there it is. I study the house. It's a square box with dull gray siding, once white, two bedrooms, a tall attic, a handful of windows on each side of it. The porch leans, rotten wood at its edges, two-by-fours as posts; it's still hanging on, empty flowerpots hanging in each corner. There's the old wicker sofa sitting there, an ashtray full of butts on the table next to it, old work boots sitting by the door. There are cobwebs on them, stretching from sole to strings; Pa hasn't used them in a while. How it is possible these same things remain in place?

I walk up to the house, feel the anger begin to warm me. I make a fist, unzip my jacket, put my hand on the back of my jeans, on my wallet full of credit cards, pick up my duffel bag. The sky above me is now filled with heavy clouds, a deep mixture of blues. I smell something sweet in the distance.

I take a deep breath and turn the handle of the door. It's late, but the house smells like greasy chicken and cigarette smoke. The dark paneling on the walls is the same, two old recliners in the same spot, a big box television in the middle of the room, the old couch with upholstery so thin you can see the bones of the couch sticking out. The wood floors are dusty, dry. The house spills light, like a box of sticks were used to put it together.

"Ma, Pa. Are you awake? It's Carmine. Listen, I got your message and . . ." I stop when I see Ma coming from the hallway that leads to the bedrooms.

She is fifty-nine, I think, but I can't be sure. Her face sags and she looks so sad, but then her blue eyes are so alive, wet and pale, there and then gone. I recognize the old dress hanging from her frame.

"Carmine, I didn't think you'd come." She puts her head down and shuffles over to me, house slippers on her feet, her long arms moving with her steps. She never stops looking at me. I stand there in the dull light, pull my cell phone out of my pocket, and begin to push buttons on it—e-mails, contacts, voice mails, there has to be something else to do in this moment.

When she hugs me, something within me curdles, but I try not to pull away immediately. I take off my jacket and lay it over the kitchen chair. My mouth dries up. The light above me swings without a lightbulb.

Ma asks me about the bus ride and about work while she puts on a pot of coffee. She's still using that old silver percolator; her reflection bounces off of it as she moves around the kitchen.

I turn around when I hear Pa coming from the hallway, slowly, a cane holding him up and his face leaning down toward the floor. I watch him move, see his body leaning to one side, halfway down to the earth already. My eyes dart toward the front door. I shift my weight in the kitchen chair, try to stay still.

"Look, Pa, Carmine made it in. He looks good, don't he?" Ma smiles that crooked smile and points a bony finger at me. The percolator spits and vibrates on the kitchen counter.

When I see his face, I feel my shoulders begin to fold in, then straighten up tall again when I feel the impulse to pounce on him, then push the feeling away, try to find something in between.

"Old man, how you doing?" I wipe the sweat from my top lip, put my hands in my pockets, look over at Ma lighting a cigarette, watching the two of us. I feel suddenly sober. I've thought of this moment for years.

For a split second, I become my former self again, knobby knees and hair over my ears, Pa at the pulpit preaching the gospel, me sitting in the pew, the smell of coffee and donuts and pamphlets behind me, Ma on the pew next to me silent. I remember the smoky smell of our house, the empty clink of forks on dinner plates, the sound of Pa snoring in his chair, the sting of his clammy hand on my face in the morning, the tattered leather of the old Bible always sitting in the center of our house.

"Carmine, son, what took you so long to get here?" He's at least three inches shorter than I remember. His clothes hang from his coat-hanger bones, a button-down shirt, old pajama bottoms; I can see the yellow whiskers growing from his cheeks. He breathes in hoarsely and gasps, moves to the living room and sits down. I sit down at the other end of the sofa.

"Pop. You look rough. Life finally getting the best of you?" I lean back on the sofa and sigh.

"Listen, boy, I'm dying. I ain't gonna do this with you." He eyes me hard, tries to straighten his spine. The congestion in his chest boils, and he begins to cough.

"Now don't start this. You haven't seen each other for fourteen years, for Christ's sake." Ma shakes her head and walks back to the kitchen.

"Can I get you something, Carmine? We don't have any of that fancy liquor you're probably used to, but we do have some of that cheap bourbon your pa used to drink." Her voice echoes and bounces off the old paneling, I can hear the hum of the old icebox, look on the walls and see my old pictures. I don't know how it's possible that time has stayed so still.

I hear Ma in the kitchen opening and closing old cabinet doors while Pa still catches his breath at the other end of the couch, his breaths short and weak; he tries to stretch them out. I can smell his oily skin, see him watching me out of his yellow eyes; we are in the wild again.

"How have things been, Pa?"

He shakes his head, sits up straight, tries to laugh before the cough grips him again.

"What's so funny?" I ask. "Is it because I'm here or you're there?" This time he doesn't laugh, looks across the room at something I don't see, and grabs his knees with his hands. His nails are overgrown, and the hair on his arms has turned gray.

"Here you go, Carmine." Ma hands me a glass of bourbon. I take a sip, slide it onto the table beside me.

"It's been a long time. I didn't think I'd ever be sitting in this room again." Ma sits in an armchair across from us and crosses her bony legs beneath her housecoat.

"It ain't normal for kids to leave home and never to come back," she says. She lights up a cigarette and stares at Pa for a long time, waiting for him to say something.

"Things have been going real good for me." I make big hand gestures as I talk, paint a real colorful picture for them. "I've just been made partner at the advertising agency I've been working at, dating a nice girl; I've got loads of money. I don't have long." I take another drink of the liquor and wince as it goes down; it tastes like it's been in the back of the cabinet for a long while.

"Your pa, he ain't got long either."

Pa starts to cough again, as though on cue, but manages to catch his breath before losing it.

"Ma, don't make this harder than it needs to be, you hear?" He tries to smile at her, but it doesn't come out right. Instead, a crooked frown appears on his face; one cheek lifting up, he almost winks.

After a minute, he pulls himself up to standing and leans on his cane. It's the only thing holding his body in place. "I'm headed to bed, boy. You stayin' or you goin'?"

Ma looks at Pa, then at me. Nothing much has changed, and she's waiting for the first swing, I think. I stand up and put my hand on my wallet, looking up at the faded white ceiling before answering.

"I think I'll crash. Is my old room open?"

CHAPTER 3

I AWAKE IN THE night to Pa screaming. I've never heard anything like it. It's a screech. No, it's more like a long, drawn-out hiss, like a siren, coming from his bones, crawling out of him. My brain doesn't know what to do with such sounds. I turn over and try to focus on the sounds of the crickets outside my window, count the women I've been with, imagine the rising and falling of the stock market, the paper I'll choose for my new resume.

In the morning, Ma is at the stove scrambling eggs. I smell the yolks harden and the whites sticking to the bottom of the pan, the salty butter melting.

"Does he always scream that way?" I stare at Ma's back as she cooks and my head aches, and I try to think about why I'm here and what I want to do.

"He has for the last month or so." Her voice is low, the way new mothers sound after being up with a newborn all night, tired, worn-out, but still resilient.

"The doctor tells us that the cancer is eatin' him up inside." She turns the pan over, dumps the eggs onto a paper plate, takes a long drag off her cigarette.

I don't have any experience with any of this. Illness. Weakness. I've been on a twelve-year happy hour, and none of it makes any sense. I think about Diego's aging face, Melanie's long, silky legs, the time we had a potluck for some account clerk's dying wife. This is the stuff from other people's lives. This isn't really life.

Outside the kitchen window, I can see the blue of a faraway mountain, remember its loneliness. I stand up to leave the room.

"Don't you want to eat?" she asks, searching my face for something familiar and knowing I'll shake my head and turn away. I barely recognize her. She's been dead to me for years.

*   *   *

My first memory of life is a little like this. There's an opening in a room full of shag carpet, some kind of hole in the floor. I fall through. Somehow her skinny arms catch me downstairs. I am safe. Other memories are harder to remember, seem scattered, disconnected. Bits of color. Flashes of light. A piece of a memory here, a feeling there. I am following her around, clinging to the backs of her legs, looking up her narrow back, calling her name. She feeds me pancakes in front of the television. She brushes the knots out of my hair; she puts me in a tub of cold water and washes my fever away. Pa brings the belt down on my back and she leaves the room. I see red. Follow her shadow. Hear her moans as she leans on the church pew and talks to Jesus. I try to put it all together and imagine a woman that I know.

* * *

A couple of hours later, I walk three blocks and find the familiar tavern easily. I walk there almost on autopilot, noting my surroundings and remembering it was the place that Pa walked to a few nights a week, to reach his disciples he told us, his belly shaking as he laughed. Neon signs blink in the windows, and I can smell the stench of air-conditioning and cigarettes as I approach the door.

I sit down at the bar. A silver Coors Light sign blinks in front of me; a layer of dust dulls the light. I remember seeing it as a child, walking up to the barstool, giving Pa a message from Ma, the sting of his hand pushing me away, my brain trying to process it.

"Hey. Take a look at my son. He's a shrimp, ain't he? God help him." His friends laugh; he doesn't turn around to look at me again. I hear the beer glass slide across the bar as I leave, hear Pa saying something about the son of Job and the trials and tribulations of his life. He spoke, and everyone turned to listen.

I tap my fingers on the bar and look around the room. The smoky air hangs, and the jukebox plays some country tune I've heard on the road somewhere. The faces look familiar: dark and weathered, but tender; there's nothing more to them than what you see here. I can smell the sour of Jack Daniels in the air and my heart quickens.

I order a beer and a shot, slide my hand through my hair, and take my jacket off. I think I'll stay awhile.

I think about my routine at home in Dallas, sitting at a bar so unlike this one. Glossy floors and high ceilings, leather chaises, the dark lights leaning in and out, the sound of money sliding across tables, deals being made, sex being bought and sold. My life was a prime-time show people live vicariously through.

The bartender looks slightly familiar to me, a tall good-looking guy I remember playing football at school. I'd go and watch the games from the sidelines, smoking weed under the bleachers or trying to sneak my hand up girls' skirts. I laugh to myself when I think about how he's still here and pushing glasses around behind a bar. Then again, how I'm still sneaking behind bleachers—only bigger ones—and chasing skirts. I still like it; it still makes sense.

"Hey, don't I know you?" I down the shot and follow it with half a glass of beer. On the jukebox, Patsy Cline swoons about love and heartache. How does that woman still have a place here?

He looks at me closely for a minute and squints. He's putting it all together. I remember his name is Adam, Adam Short.

"It's Carmine, right?" He leans over the bar in my direction and looks at me, tries to find any memories stored, things we might have shared.

"Yes, Carmine St. Clair. I think we went to school together a long time ago." I drink the last of my beer and tap the glass on the bar. He fills it up from the tap and dries his hand on a towel.

"You haven't been around these parts in years, have you? Seems like I'd remember seeing you around. You're big-city now, aren't you?"

I smile. Lean back in my chair. Tell him about all the money I've made in Dallas and how I won't be here for long, that I'm only stopping in to check on my folks on my way to the East Coast to make some more coins.

"You know how it is," I tell him. "I can't believe you're still working at this bar. Didn't your pop used to serve drinks to mine back in the day?" A jukebox switches songs, something by the Rolling Stones, and I hear the pinball machine clicking somewhere in the room.

"Yep, still here, like a lot of us. Your folks have been struggling the last few years, I hear." He turns a sink on behind the bar and starts washing a glass.

"Ain't been a whole lot happening in these parts for any of us, but after the church, your Pa couldn't seem to stay out of trouble. But I'm sure you know about all of that." He dries the glass and then dips another one into the sudsy water.

He keeps talking for a long time and tells me how Pa's had some trouble with some folks around town, how Ma's been in the food line at the charity, how some of the winters have been harsh.

"Sounds like they made it all right," I say, tipping my empty glass toward him again. "Only Pa is sick now." I look around the room behind me, but only see a few scattered faces, no one I recognize. "I'm just not sure what that has to do with me, you know?" I reach down the bar and grab a bowl of peanuts, toss a few in my mouth. They taste like the bar smells. It's something to do.

"My pa passed away a few years ago, left me this bar. Sometimes I find myself waiting for him to come out of the cooler, a case of beer in his arms. It's tough, man, tough, and now my mother can't take care of herself, needs help with the simplest of things. It's a strange position for a man to be in, a strange feeling to get used to. I still don't know what I'm doing." He drains the sink and folds the towel, his eyes turned in.

"Why is that?" I ask him. He looks at me strangely, as though he suddenly doesn't recognize me, like I've just walked up to him, a new face in the crowd.

Just then a group of men come up to the bar and order drinks, a rowdy group; they fill in the voids and the room has become something else. I slide my coat on and walk out. When the cold mountain air hits me, I remember I'm not in Dallas anymore.

CHAPTER 4

FOR THE FIRST COUPLE of days, it all feels so mechanical. Little stick figures walking about, changes in scenes, background noise; it all seems so separate from anything I know about. Ma shuffling in and out of their bedroom, Pa's moans, the *Price Is Right* on the TV, then later in the evening, *Wheel of Fortune*, the clink of his spoon hitting the bowl of oatmeal he eats before bed.

The sounds of his pain seem cyclical—they are the worst at night, die off in the mornings, but then come back in the afternoon around lunch. I pop a couple of muscle relaxers in the day and try to coast through it, my body jelly, my mind still in Dallas, in the clouds, still on top. I don't know what I'm doing here but doing time, waiting for the next wave to catch.

At night when all the lights are off in the house, I sit out on the front porch. I can't believe how quiet it is in these mountains, how silently everything grows and grows until green covers everything, but then nothing changes and things stay the same beneath it all, a picture book that repeats the same images, flipping one after the other.

Through conversations in the hallway, Ma tells me that Pa's cancer started in his colon, swam and grew until it thrived in all of his lymph glands; now there are tumors in his lungs, one growing in his brain. He has blood clots in his legs and he probably won't walk much longer.

"How long has this been going on?" I ask her as she folds laundry into piles on the kitchen table.

"Oh, you know, Carmine, your pa don't like to go to the doctor much. Never has. I had a feeling something was up. He was eating like a horse, but dropping weight like . . . I don't know. By the time I'd convinced him to see someone, it was just about too late to do anything." She turns around and stirs something on the stove and then pulls out a chair.

"What are we talking here, Ma? A week, a couple of years? Isn't there some kind of treatment? Money doesn't matter; I'll pay for it."

She cuts me off. "No, Carmine, there isn't. Money hasn't got anything to do with this. You ain't been around in years, and I don't know how much you care for him, but I thought you should know. That's why I called."

"I've got some calls to make," I tell her and stand up and leave the room. Down the hall, Pa's old TV yells my old commercials to the room.

*   *   *

My father was meant for a life in the sun, running the family's fishing business, his skin already so beaten and worn, he belonged on a boat, at the sea, salt in his mouth. He grew up in Texas, worked his father's fishing business, shrimp, crabs, the Gulf's seafood, until his father gambled and drank it all away, the boat, the connections, eventually his life.

I remember Grandpa well. He would come to family dinners, bottle in hand, already half-crocked by half-day. I thought he was funny, charismatic, gritty. I sat near him always, trying to get a whiff of his alcohol-heavy breath; it was as sweet as honey, endearing. It was love and tenderness, and as necessary as Christmas and the first day of school. Ceremonial, yet rotten and weak.

His clothes were always dirty and weathered, but he worked every day of his life. People grew accustomed to him being drunk. I began to think it was okay after all, though deep down I was ashamed of them all.

After Grandpa passed, Pa came to Eton to find a few distant relatives, found work, mostly odd jobs, roofing, carpentry, plumbing in the palm of the Appalachians, and life went on.

He met Ma on an old logging road when he was just twenty-two years old. The two of them were like magnets, he told me, so drawn to one another. He was doing some day labor with a wood company; she was there with her father, taking notes about wood grades and insect development, shielding her eyes from the sun and watching the men work.

"She was quiet as a mouse, boy. I worried if I clapped my hands too loudly, she'd fall apart." He laughed and looked across the room to her, pretended to clap, waved his hands instead. "But she's stronger than she looks."

They were married a few months after they met. They lived in a series of run-down apartments before Pa earned enough to buy this house at an auction. I came along less than a year later, unplanned, but they said they were ready to try their hand at raising a family.

Pa grew up poor, spending whole days and sometimes nights floating in that fishing boat on the Texas coast, the sun leathering his face, his father telling him about the ways of the world and how you had to take advantage of the world before it took advantage of you. Ma came from more stability. My grandparents lived and worked the forest, but there wasn't anything ever said and the liquor ran through the house like water. Sundays they all sat on the cold hard pews in Eton, miles apart, and prayed, but they could never say for just what.

Ma and Pa make it seem like their early years together were good—that there was love and enough to get by and when the money grew short they didn't mind because they had each other. Sometimes they'd wait until it got real dark and they'd enter the fields of some of the orchards and steal apples and pull blueberries off the bushes in handfuls.

It lasted awhile. Neither of them had ever been happier, but they didn't trust it. They knew life was waiting just around the corner to get them, to take it all away, so they made sure they were ready.

For a while, Pa talked about going back to Texas to rebuild the fishing business, to build some real roots, to leave Ma's past behind her and start something new.

"But we knew there wasn't nothing back there in Texas for us, but a boat with a hole in it and some old debts from Granddaddy. I figured that wasn't no way to start anything new, not with the past hanging on so hard."

They decided to stay in Eton, and Pa found Jesus soon after, became a preacher, joking that there had to be more money in saving souls than in fishing. The small Baptist church up the road from our house needed a leader and it was enough. The rest of the time he built furniture: cribs and rocking chairs, dressers, chests of hope, whatever some of the locals or tourists passing through wanted. He spent hours in his shed, shaping and twisting the softwood of Georgia into dreams, the glue and booze keeping him in a calm trance. Ma and I would sometimes watch him through the windows of his workshop behind our house and wonder who he really was, searching the clouds for the next storm, trying to stay away from each other.

"He wasn't always like this, Carmine," she used to tell me. "He used to be sweet; he treated me like a queen when we was first married. Then something just died inside of him. When you came along he was so happy, but then he started remembering all these bad things that happened to him when he was a boy, all those beatings, and how his Pa would leave him places, sometimes on the water, sometimes in the middle of a field, sometimes with family he barely knew. And then times was real tough here in Eton, and there was never enough money and never enough work, and I tried, Carmine. I wanted him to be good to us."

*   *   *

Later that night, I sit at the dinner table with them, push around stew in a plastic bowl, listen to Pa clear his throat. It sounds exaggerated. His Bible rests near his bowl. When he opens it up and starts flipping through the pages, I think I'll snap.

"Still pretending, huh, Pa?" I pick up my glass of water, tip it back, drink the whole thing, but stare at him the whole time.

I hear the thump of that Bible in my mind as though it was yesterday. His voice resonates: "The Sins of the fathers shall be visited upon seven generations of the sons." He also liked Isaiah 14:21—"Prepare a place to slaughter his sons for the sins of their forefathers; they are not to rise to inherit the land and cover the earth with their cities."

He stares back at me until his eyes begin to water and he looks away.

"I never was any good at pretending, boy." He closes his Bible and slides it to the middle of the table. I take another tablespoon of pasty stew and then push the bowl away.

Ma's shoulders tighten. She picks up our bowls and starts the old percolator again.

"Carmine, your pa is too sick for trouble. I mean it. He don't need any trouble." She sighs into her own chest and rinses the bowls in the sink.

If I heard it once, I heard it a thousand times. "That boy has got to learn to be a man, to relinquish his sins, and goddamn it, I'm gonna make sure of it."

"I know he ain't right," I'd hear Ma whisper to someone, "but don't a man have a right to teach his son any way he sees fit?" I heard her say it on the phone more than once.

"I didn't come here to make trouble, Ma, but a man has got to be himself, doesn't he? Isn't that what you always said, Pa? Something about marching to the beat of your own drum or something?" I smile. Pull a cigarette out of Ma's pack and light it up. It's getting dark outside and I can see the fireflies fly past the window.

"Since when do you smoke?" he asks. Ma serves him a cup of coffee with milk, the way he likes it. His breathing is labored, and he stares at the cup as though it's a chore to consider it.

I remember the time he caught me smoking and how I thought he'd let me get away with it because he didn't say anything for days. It was something most of the kids did. My friends and I'd steal cigarettes from our mothers' purses and smoke them out by those old tracks while we waited for the train to pass. One time Pa was driving by, slowed his car to a creep, and looked right at me.

But then it came up. I should have known he wouldn't let me get away with it. He never let anything slide. Ma and Pa were fighting over money—there was never enough—when he brought it up. Furniture brought in a little, church contributions helped, but it wasn't enough to get by. Some late nights we'd drive from dumpster to dumpster and collect things people threw away, fix and sell them. Pa felt so ashamed about this. What would people think if they saw the town's preacher digging through their trash?

I remember the brightness of my bedroom light snapping on in the middle of the night when their voices had died down, and the pound of his steps moved closer; they seemed to shake the whole house. "Boy, get up out of that bed; do it now. It's about time you and I had a talk about some of your choices, man-to-man, don't you think?" He slapped me across my face, pulled me up straight beside him, held his hand over my mouth to get me to stop hyperventilating.

"Now stop it, stop it right now. You ain't got nothing to cry about, boy. I just want to talk to you a minute." I smelled the sour whiskey coming from his mouth as he talked late into the night, punctuating lectures with slaps, telling me about what it means to be a hardworking, God-fearing man.

I lean across the table and get close to him; he smells like old bones, rotten eggs, the bottom of those old dumpsters.

"I smoke when I want to, always did. You got something to say about that, old man?" I pull another cigarette from the pack and light it up. Think about blowing the smoke into his face, but don't.

"Oh, you're Mr. Big Shot now, are you?" He calmly lifts the mug up to his mouth and takes a drink; his hand shakes as he sets it back down on the table. "No kind of son leaves his folks and don't come back. Stomp me if you want to. I can't stop you. But it won't change anything. I'm dying, you fool."

I hear a fire truck pass a few blocks away and the song of an owl's hoot.

"Who's gonna save the preacher, Pa? Jesus?" I stub the cigarette out in the ashtray, half-smoked.

He looks at me for a long time and I try not to blink. The whites of his eyes have a yellow hue to them, delicate like a baby's skin; his skin hangs and moves when he breathes hard. He starts to say something, but then a storm of phlegm takes him over.

I get up and walk out of the room. The sight of him so weak and helpless saddens and disgusts me.

*   *   *

"Hey, Diego, it's Carmine. Listen, I want to be a part of the next big thing; whatever it is, I'm with you. I'm taking care of some personal business right now, but I can be back in Dallas within a day. Call me back."

I flip the phone closed and scroll through my contacts; there's no one else, there'd only been Icarus, Diego, one plan.

I keep my cell phone in my hand, carry it around the house with me, but it never rings, it never even rings. So many relationships and pursuits and sex and deals, and my phone never rings. Not even Melanie. I believe it must be temporary.

Throughout the day I pick up the phone and try to think of someone else to call, don't know who it would be, put the phone down and stare out into the black of the street I grew up on, the square houses across the street, the broken streetlight with a shoe dangling from it, the old railroad tracks. How it all came to be.

In Dallas, everything was illusion and insulation. A penthouse in the sky filled with shiny substance: the leather sofa, the fine linens, the original art that hung on the wall in dark frames, Versace and Cuisinart and high-end electronic systems of every kind, stainless steel and black matte catching all angles of the light, Nintendo, Sony, a large-screen TV, more, trophies everywhere—there was never enough. I know I stood in line to buy these things or spent drunken nights on the phone with catalog reps, credit card in hand, filling every second with something. "Thank you for calling The Sharper Image, may I help you?" was music to my ears. Stuff fueled the fire within, filling me, encouraging me to gather and own more, allowing me to forget, keeping the guilt a few steps behind me.

There was always something new around, something shipped, tag just removed, unused and uncertain. In my closet there were rows of expensive suits hanging lifeless on cold hangers, underneath, fifty pairs of shoes. The furniture, the suede chaise, a decadent chocolate mohair sofa with luxe and rich pillows, cork-top coffee and side tables, pearl walls paired with Robert Hansen artwork, handmade mahogany bookcases custom-carved to hold my large collection of record albums, terrazzo floors throughout the penthouse, sumptuous cream Flokati and Peruvian rugs, large sash windows that overlooked the Dallas sky, and a plush ceiling finished in elegant, satin-brass recessed lights. I got amorous looking at all of that stuff—mine, all of it mine. I wanted to come on my things, mark my territory, paddle my chests with my fists. I was finally in control, over the top. I had rewritten history; Eton was fucking bad fiction.

In the kitchen, shiny new appliance after appliance that would never be used lined the backs of my countertops with names like Frigidaire, Novell, Bosch. I never ate at home, never used the kitchen or the refrigerator, barely the bathroom or bedroom. I didn't want to taint any of it. I wanted to keep it all somehow separate from me, clean and protected and beyond the reaches of human stains. I never actually lived in my own life.

But it all meant nothing to me. Simultaneously, I prayed for fire and more things, arson and more money. I dreamed of partner status. Glory. Another wedge between me and my past. I got further and further from the back of Pa's hand, the shiny metal of those railroad tracks, the orange Georgia soil.

*   *   *

"Carmine, you awake?" Ma's voice is quieter than I remember. I see the shadow of her form peeking in my doorway.

For days I've been avoiding both of them, coming out at night, waiting until I could tell them when I'd be leaving and what I'd be doing next.

I've got a handful of ideas. A few Icarus contacts. Thoughts of heading out west or east and starting fresh. Maybe even cutting loose of it all and buying a fishing boat somewhere like Mexico. Taking care of a sick old man I never really liked ain't in my plans.

"Carmine, I know none of this is easy for you and we ain't on the best of terms, but I need your help. I'm so tired, and your old man needs you." She stands there for a few minutes and then I hear her feet sliding across the wood floor, then the squeak of her sitting down at the end of my bed.

"I'm not the person I was, Ma. I'm not, and to me, Pa is the same old son of a bitch he always was. I got nothing for him. I came for you."

She clears her throat, and I can see the profile of her face when she turns toward the window. A small ray of light reaches in from the streetlight and casts her face in it. I notice how her shoulders bend in toward her chest, how she's caving in, how the skin on her neck sags.

"Carmine, you got to leave the past where it is."

"Why would I do that, Ma? If you leave the past alone, it's bound to sneak up on you. You should know that." I get up from the bed and go sit in the corner chair. I need distance to think.

"Boy, if that were true, we'd all be in bigger trouble than this. I'm tired. I'm going back to bed." She stands up and looks at me for a long time before walking out of the room.

She's wrong and I know it. You've got to stay one step ahead in the game. Otherwise, you lose.

CHAPTER 5

THE NEXT AFTERNOON, I'M sitting at the tavern again, staring at the white blinking light of the Coors Light sign. I swallow a whole draft beer in two drinks and order another one. I scan the room for women. Tug on the belt loop of my jeans. Tap my foot.

When I walked out the front door earlier, Ma was in the front yard watering the plants. She watched me, waited for me to speak. When I got to the gate and opened it, she turned off the water and called my name.

"You didn't come back here because you needed a place to stay; I know it ain't like that. I need help getting your pa in and out of bed, in and out of the car for doctors' appointments. I've been handling it alone for a long time, and that's why we called, see? He ain't got long, Carmine, he ain't got long."

I stared at her for a long time, followed the short lines that darted out on both sides of her eyes, looked at the creases around her mouth, the gray that sliced through her golden hair. The sun felt hot on my face, and I squinted.

"Listen, Ma, I don't owe that man anything, or you for that matter." I closed the gate behind me and walked quickly down the sidewalk without looking back. No one was going to tell me what I needed to do, what I needed to be, especially not her and not for him. Things were gonna happen, be what they'd be, regardless of what I did. That's how it always was, how it'd always be.

*   *   *

I sip on the draft beer and remember the funeral services Pa used to preside over. Sometimes he had me come to the church to help set up chairs or hand out programs. I remember the dead faces peeking out of coffins, the gray skin with color painted on, the smell of the funeral flowers filling the room.

I'd see him standing at the front of the sanctuary, watching me, his hands on his hips. His voice filled the whole room, bouncing off the walls, hitting me in my chest, making people rise from their seats and chant some kind of song.

"Fear not, for I have redeemed you; I have called you by your name; you are Mine. When you pass through the waters, I will be with you; and through the rivers, they shall not overflow you. When you walk through the fire, you shall not be burned."

I'd watch Pa's lips move as he spoke, wonder what these words meant. If he was both the Savior and the flames scorching me, who would save me?

I see a young blonde sitting in the corner of the room. I've finished a fifth beer, my belly is full, I feel preyful and alive, I know there's not anything I can't do. Pa's cough, Ma's caving chest have been pushed to a closed corner of my mind. I have money, I have good looks, I have power, Pa is almost dead, what could stop me?

I walk up to the table, ask to sit down; she tells me she's waiting for a friend. She's in her mid-twenties, pale hair and eyes. I feel like I can melt her skin just by looking at it. I imagine my hands on her breasts, her sweet breath on my neck, the protruding bones of her lower back as I lower her onto me. A collector, that's what I am. A cultivator, a curator, I love beautiful things I can own. It makes sense now.

I sit. "Can I keep you company while you wait? I'd love to buy you a drink to make the time pass easier." I smile, slide into the booth next to her, wave the waitress over and start my performance.

I tell her that I'm in town from Dallas and that I've just made partner at my firm and that my pa is dying and that I'm taking it real hard. I see the pity form in her eyes; her edges soften. I lean my head down a little to show that I hurt; I try not to laugh out loud.

Her tenderness is almost insulting. Her hair and eyes so soft, she hasn't seen enough of the world to protect herself from the likes of me. I can't help it. It's what I do. Do lions feel bad for hunting?

She leans closer to me, demure. She is not completely without a price; she's doing what she does too. I feed her drinks and pretend the rest of the world doesn't exist. Out of the corner of my eye, I see the bartender looking at me. I nod.

I convince her that I could use a friend and that her friend won't mind waiting awhile for her. I take her hand, ask her to take a walk with me. I feel the familiar scent of Eton air as we walk up and down the deserted streets of downtown and talk about her life as a new RN. She has family here in Eton and doesn't come up much, she says. I listen, grab her hand, make a fist with my other hand. I feel impatient.

"It's such a beautiful night, Carmine, isn't it?" She holds my hand tighter and looks off into the distance. A few blocks away an old church bell chimes; it sounds familiar. I remember walking these streets as a teenager, see the trees I used to sit under and smoke. Across the street there's the old movie theater where I kissed my first girls, held small clammy hands. I can't hear or see the old train, but I know it's close. Why does everything stay so still like this?

I pull her close under a streetlight, lean her against the brick wall of Smith's drugstore, bring my lips close to hers and hover, tell her that I just need to be close to someone and that she seems like such a nice person and that I bet she makes a good nurse.

"It's like we were supposed to meet, like it's fate," she says as she hugs me back.

I nod, slip my hand under her coat, pretend that I'm back in Dallas and I've got a life to go back to, that this right here can be something more than what it's always been.

Twenty minutes later I am fucking her in the backseat of her car. I push inside of her hard, feel her writhe and moan beneath me; she wants me. I make it count. The Corolla rocks with us and sings. I spread her legs and start talking in her ear, push my weight on her, rest on top of her for a few moments. The plastic molding of the backseat rubs my head, and I feel so tired all of a sudden, so out of it, as though the last fourteen years of my life are sitting on my shoulders.

"Can you feel that?" I ask her. "Does it hurt?" I feel such a conflict within—I equally want to hold her, equally want to hurt her, damage her, make someone see what it's like here within.

"Slow down, please," she says. I can feel her squirm beneath me, try to catch her breath. She's the gazelle and I'm the bitter wild.

"Don't you like it like that?" I move in deeper and pause, put my arms around her, beneath her.

"I don't know . . ." Her voice sounds childish and weak, another girl behind the bleachers. Why do they always act like they didn't come here of their own free will?

I put my face in her hair, breathe her in. She smells bitter to me, so untrustworthy, almost rank. I lean up and push her knees forward.

I think I hear her crying softly below me, but she pulls me closer, buries her head into my neck. Outside, a few cars pass and a plane flies overhead. I am out of my body again and somewhere else. The next half hour passes like a cloud of smoke, slowly, time swallowing itself.

"When can I see you again?" she asks as I step out of the car and straighten my clothes, smell the tips of my fingers and clear my throat. I offer to walk her back to the bar so she can meet her friend, but I just want to be done with it.

"I don't know," I say as she steps out onto the sidewalk. I light a cigarette and get a good look at her. The small pink cardigan she wears, the pearl earrings, the jeans and sensible shoes. Something about her reminds me of Ma—maybe the light olive tone of her skin or the way her hips protrude out of her jeans. I shudder.

"I have never done anything like this, but I feel like we have a real connection here, don't you?" She smoothes her hair and looks at me.

Yes, I tell her, we do, and then I agree when she says it's special and that we have real potential and that when something like this comes along you've got to do something about it.

She keeps on talking, but I can't make out any of her words anymore. We've known each other two hours now, and I can't remember her name, can't quite place her, feel like everything is moving in slow motion or maybe not at all.

We walk the same two blocks back to the bar, and when we get there, I open the door for her, wait as she steps in, and then start walking the opposite direction.

"Wait," she says, and I wave my hand. "I've got to be going," I tell her, "but you be good."

*   *   *

It is after midnight when I walk back into the house. I feel hollow. I haven't eaten much in days, a handful of cocktail peanuts, a candy bar from the vending machine at the bus station. I am running on fumes.

I can smell the girl's skin on me, sweet and green like fresh peas. She was too easy; done it again. Is this all that I really am?

My head spins from the beer, and the house is so quiet. I stumble to my bedroom, sit on the bed, and put my head in my hands; feel myself begin to sweat. I pick up my phone; no missed calls, there is no one coming for me and there is nowhere for me to be.

I lay my head back on my pillow, think about Pa laying in his bed just a few feet away. I can smell the yellow stench of a body decaying—is it his or mine?

I remember those funerals, the one dead person in the room, the taste of suffering, those lines of scripture floating in the air.

"Let not your heart be troubled; you believe in God, believe also in Me." Pa read me this piece of scripture after I fell off the jungle gym at the park near our house and broke my arm. I remember the piercing pain traveled up and down my body as he spoke. I fought back tears and watched the pupils of his eyes expand and retract as he sat and watched me suffer.

Three days later he took me to the hospital for a cast and told me that I now knew salvation and what it means to pay for my sins, to suffer for them.

You pay the price now, Pa, don't you? How does it feel?

Chapter 6

The next morning I am pounding the keys of an old typewriter I found in the closet. At the top of the page, Huemanity Creative, the name of my company, is all I have for my business plan so far.

I can hear the clink of Pa's spoon in the next room and it is distracting; sometimes he can't swallow and Ma feeds him like an infant. I hear her speak to him in small fuzzy words.

I can't place any of it, this new reality. I can't grab hold of it. It slips from my hands. I don't know what it means. I have to keep myself from running in there and telling him that we know he's going to attack again at any minute. But I don't.

Outside my bedroom window I see the tiny wings of a mockingbird flying around the empty feeder, searching. I throw my pen at the glass pane.

I pull on a pair of old sweats, find my tennis shoes sitting under my bed, and slide them on. I've got to get away from the sounds and the smells.

My feet hit the sidewalk outside of the house hard and firm, and I begin to jog methodically, one bent leg in front of the other, first slowly, then I find a delicate pace and rhythm.

I haven't gone running since high school when I was on the track team. I can remember the feel of the orange gravel of the track beneath my feet, see the blurry faces of people in the bleachers as I passed them, hear the whistle of the coach. I never pursued it again, never wanted to attend meets, I just wanted to run. I stopped when I turned sixteen and got a job at the local pizza joint.

In Dallas, the mornings were too heavy from the night before to think about running; it was enough to put on my costume and rehearse my lines.

I run around the block, make one big square, hear the wind chimes on people's porches, a lawn mower in the distance, watch pinwheels turn in lawns, and shield my eyes from the sun.

I try to make a mental list of clients in my head. Who would I hustle? Who could I get to join me? I can't keep my mind on the task, but I begin to feel euphoric under my feet. My chest burns; I heave and try to catch my breath. I am moving, I am young again, I can start over.

I keep running, don't look up and notice my surroundings, watch the tips of my toes and notice how Eton fades into the background.

I stop running when my feet hit Douglas Street and I realize where I am. I stand across the street from the railroad tracks. They are no longer used, rusty and red from the weather, swollen; they'll never go away. Across the street, the houses dilapidated and lean. The winters here are harsh; people have migrated to places with more work. Seems like everything can be summed up like that. A small fact, a blip in history, a simple explanation for a lifetime of pain.

Where the warehouse once sat, there's a big empty lot, a soft shell of foundation that once held the big aluminum building. Someone has drug a few lawn chairs into the center. One of them is turned over; it's become some kind of meeting place.

I lean down and put my hands on my knees and try to catch my breath; my chest burns. I don't remember feeling so awake; there is blood in my veins. I can feel my toes, the pounding in the back of my head. I have never been so aware of my own boundaries.

My eyes search the scene for the light pole near the tracks, silver and dull. I expect to see our bikes leaning up against it, the old beer bottle rolling down the hill. Then the black boy's smooth head laying on the gravel ground inside the warehouse.

I've done my best not to think of that night for the last nearly twenty years, to overlook it, to pretend it wasn't me at all, or that it didn't actually matter. Sometimes I play it out differently—I run across the street, shout at the teenagers, pull the boy up, figure out how to make it right for everyone, and I save him. He lives. But then I realize, and I've always realized, that I'm as bad as the thing I saw done, the things I've done with my own hands, and there ain't nothing I can do about those either. All us St. Clairs are the same.

I can feel the sweat run down my back, study the old building and the tracks and the clouds above. I sit on the edge of the curb and try to push my thoughts back to the client list. I've got to build a ladder to the top again because there's nothing down here at the bottom but this. Guilt, broken bones, a merciless God, struggle.

I kick a few rocks with my feet and run through a list of names in my mind: Jennifer, Rick, Alex, Hector—they all worked at Icarus and have to be doing something. I try to think of the other clients we serviced; there were just a handful: Tropical Convenience Stores, Kitchens R Us, The Dance Factory. There wasn't enough to keep even one of us in business. The Carmichael account brought in 90 percent of the money and kept us all alive.

My mind wanders again, and I think of myself that night. There's a tall magnolia tree a block away, and I can smell its fragrance, remember smelling it that night, wet with dew.

"Say something, why don't you say something?" I yell at him, kick his limp leg, watch his body laying on its side.

"Stop being stupid and get up," I yell at him, watch the blood roll down his forehead onto the ground. Hear the voices of the kids somewhere in the distance, somewhere far down the train tracks. Wonder why no one was there to save us.

I was at the kitchen table eating a bowl of Cheerios when Pa read the newspaper article to Ma as she chopped up onions and carrots and poured them into the Crock-Pot with the roast. I can smell the gravy forming in the pot, hear the water rolling down the sink drain. My muscles hurt from straining, the tension of holding it in the last few days.

"His mother went looking for him around midnight that night, found him on the ground inside that old warehouse. Police think some teenagers—probably white ones—killed him with a broken bottle or rock or something, but they don't know who."

"Them nigger boys ought to know better than to be out at night like that," Ma says without turning around. "It just ain't safe for them around here."

Pa turns his newspaper over and folds it in half. I watch him from across the table, study his face, see myself in the lens of his glasses; my reflection is pale and transparent. I am an illusion of light. Pa made it seem so righteous to be wrong.

*   *   *

I am nearly home when I take a sharp left and jog to the Baptist church Pa preached at. It stands barren and raw, the old clapboard siding missing pieces, the paint chipping, the aluminum gutters falling and barely hanging on; it is just as I remember. On the marquee, the message says Jesus Saves. I follow the lines of the black magnetic letters; the S in Saves has slipped, hangs almost sideways. I smile. Pa never would have let that happen, I think. He said God was in the details.

I stand in front of the small building. On the other side of it, the sun is beginning to set; it's a pale orange now, hovers just above the building, giving it an ominous glow. I walk up the stairs to the church and try to open the door, but it is locked. I stand at the top of the stairs and look around. I don't understand how so little could have changed in the past fourteen years. Across the street an old abandoned gas station sits, leaning and oblong. It has sat like this for years, the old gas pumps dangling from their holsters, the square metal boxes scavenged and disassembled for their scrap parts. The red paint of the building hangs on, then is stripped to white in spots; there are potholes in the parking lot.

Next door to the church there are a few houses, white metal siding, flowerpots hanging at each corner; they all look alike. In the distance, I can smell someone's dinner cooking, spaghetti; farther away, a barbeque grill burns. In Dallas, it seemed like there were so few details, nothing but a rush of people and energy, things out of reach. Fast cars, a few blazing taillights, brick buildings, waiters with long white aprons, a patch of grass or an ornate tree next to my building, car horns, and mannequins dressed with expensive clothing.

I sit on the stairs of the church until I see the light come on in the building and hear the click of the lock slide open. My legs burn from the run; I can feel my muscles stretch under my skin. I crave an anesthetic. Life comes on you so fast when you're sober; you feel everything.

When I step inside the building, I can smell the coffee brewing. That was always Ma's job, to take care of all the preparations, refreshments, making sure the floors were Pine-Soled, the programs crisp and fresh from the printers.

I walk up to the front of the church, run my hands along the pews as I approach the altar. I stare at the cross and try to see it as something more than two pieces of wood crossing each other, more than man's feelings of guilt about himself. I slow down when I see a vision of Pa at the pulpit. I stop, look, see his face there, wanting and challenging me. I keep moving toward him.

"Service doesn't start for another hour, son." I turn around and see a short, bald black man enter the room. The little bit of hair above his ears is white and fuzzy, his suit a dark navy blue; the tips of his shoes shine. Pa always wore black, running the lint brush up and down his clothes every time he stepped out of the house, his shoes a beaten brown leather; he always had a full head of thick hair.

"Hello, yes, I know. My father used to be the preacher here. This place was a second home to me. It hasn't changed much, has it?" Pa hadn't been there in at least ten years, I know. He stopped when his bones started hurting too much and the congregation dwindled to just a few people, those that refused to believe Pa was anything but what he'd said he was.

"No, things haven't changed much here, although we're a congregation of 130 now." He walks toward me, and I can see him more clearly now. He's not that old, just a little past fifty; his gait is proud, and he smiles at me.

He asks about Pa and about our family, and when I tell him he nods, although I can't tell if he knows of us or not.

I look at the cross again and the empty pulpit. I can feel something in my bones, like the weather is changing. My stomach turns; I feel hot behind my eyes.

"Are all sins measured the same? How long do we have to pay a price for something we did or didn't do?" I yell across the room at him and wait for him to turn around. My voice is high and loud. He shifts the Bible from one hand to the other. The light bounces off the shine of his head. He turns around and looks at me for a long time before he says anything.

"There is God, and then there is everything else. All you need to do is ask for forgiveness for whatever it is and offer the same to others."

"If all we have to do is ask for God's forgiveness every time we do something wrong, what's the point of living right at all then?" I am angry all of a sudden. I rock back and forth in my shoes and wait for him to answer. I look at him long and hard, dare him, beg him to come closer.

"Aren't you going to minister to me, minister?" I walk and stand right in front of him. My fists clench and I eye him hard.

"Listen, services will be starting soon, and I invite you to worship with us. If you'd like to make an appointment with me, I'd be glad to sit with you and answer some of your questions." He doesn't blink, but his eyes are soft and kind and wet at the edges. His hand rests on the pinewood of the pew. He is not afraid and I can't understand why.

I walk out the front door of the church, push the door hard so that it makes a sucking, final sound.

I walk down the stairs slowly, and my legs feel so weak beneath me; I am famished. I have never felt so hungry in my life. My mouth waters and I search for the smells from earlier, pick up my pace, and walk past the white houses. The smells have faded, but I look inside the windows of the houses at TVs blaring, recliners with people in them, hear kids playing in their backyards, see a couple on their porch holding hands. Life here seems so simple, yet so complicated.

CHAPTER 7

I AM SLEEPING DEEP, so deep I can hear Pa's voice in the distance. It is acrylic and dry. He is young and I can see his broad shoulders, vast hands, hear the sound of his booted feet. I am dreaming my own memories. Outside, I hear the big, billowing horn of a boat, smell salt in the air, look around and see clutter: ashtrays full of cigarette butts, empty food cartons, rolled-up socks, a Tonka truck, a handful of Legos. Outside the window, I see the U-Haul truck in front of the house, the back of it open.

"I ain't dealing with it no more, Ron, you make it too hard. Something's got to change or our boy ain't gonna come out right. I've got to save you or us, and I'm starting to get the feeling that even Jesus himself can't save you." Through the crack of my bedroom door, I see her in the kitchen with her hands on her bony hips, her light hair pulled back in a ponytail at the bottom of her neck. She's making a bunch of sandwiches on the table, buttering all the pieces of bread with mayonnaise before putting them down again, adding slices of bologna two at a time.

Pa sits at the table drinking a cup of coffee. He is calm; he swooshes the cup around and makes circles with the coffee in the bottom of the cup.

"Virginia, you aren't going anywhere. How would it look if the town's preacher's wife left him? You think you can raise that boy alone? Where you gonna go? You think your people are gonna take you and that boy in? All I've been trying to do is put the fear of God in him so that he comes out good and godly, and you wanna walk around here like I'm some kind of animal."

He goes on to tell her that she can't survive without him, that she's nearly helpless anyhow, that he's the boy's father and that he knows right from wrong, that he's going by the Holy Book, and that it's the only way, says that's how his pa did it. "If he knows how to hurt now, it'll be easier for him later in life. Life is painful, Virginia, and you know it." She slides into the chair across from him, rubs her hands up and down her cheek, rests her face in her hands.

From the doorway, I am hopeful, I believe she might finally save me, might finally be turning over in her sleep. I wait for her to say something; I wait for so long, I twist and turn because I have to use it.

When I get out of the bathroom, I sneak closer to the kitchen, hide behind an old sitting chair, hear her whisper that she just doesn't want her son to hate her and that she'll stay and pray that he's doing right by them.

The next memory I have is that inky stretch of night, the colored boy's face, the feel of the starch of my bedsheets on my wet face when I crawled into bed that night.

*   *   *

I open my bedroom door in time to see him wobble to the bathroom. For a second or two, I watch him, how the old man nearly has to drag his legs each step, how he leans on the old paneling for support, how each breath is labored and hard and long and wet.

The empty pages of my business plan scatter across my bed; the list of my old colleagues falls to the floor. I feel like I've never actually left this room and that Dallas is just a mirage.

I start to walk down the hall toward the kitchen, stop a few feet away as he falls to the floor. It feels like it's all happening in slow motion; I wait for time to catch up and resume normal speed. His legs fold beneath him. He doesn't cry out for help, but his breathing is so loud, the phlegm holds onto the walls of his lungs, drags on the bottom like sandpaper on a wood floor; heavy, it keeps him down on the floor. He grasps at the doorway; his fingernails dig into the wood, but he's not strong enough to get up.

I continue to watch. It's a spectacle; he looks like a bunch of bones in a yellow pillowcase, and I don't recognize him. I look down the hallway hoping to see Ma. Time catches up and I stand up straight, my legs no longer soft.

"Pop? Do you need some help?" I start to walk toward him; he grabs at his cane that's fallen a foot away, but he can't reach it.

He waves his hand at me, pushing me away. "I got it. I don't need any help from you." He's focused on his body, what it can and cannot do. There is no world beyond this hallway—he, me, the space between us, this is both the milestone and the mile itself.

"Listen, Pop, just let me help you up." I walk closer to him, but when I get there I don't know what to do; a small smile forms on my face—it comes from somewhere deep.

It throws me back to this one day. I had been playing on a tree outside, alone. The limb was wet and I fell to the ground on my back and the air had been knocked out of me completely, my throat was dry. I think I broke my elbow, the pain so piercing and ripe. I didn't want Ma or Pa to find out so I kept it to myself, but during dinner as I carried my plate to the table, pain shot through my arm and I dropped my food and the plate shattered on the wood floor in the kitchen. Pa immediately picked me up and threw me across the room. It was just like that—seemingly so easy for him.

He used to collect odd things—clocks, and more—his prized possession was a 1000-watt light bulb that he had found. When he threw me I fell on it and it shattered, a piece of it stuck in the skin right under my heart leaving the 'x-shaped' scar that I wouldn't want to live without now. It is who I am.

The memory comes back in fragments: burning skin, the smell of a rotting human soul, a thunderstorm raging outside, hot metal used to brand furniture, a customer that didn't pay his bill, mom cowered in the corner. The pieces tell a story. Her voice. His strength. A lethal combination. Her words, the son of bitches, the morons, the worthless piece of shits, all of the names hurt just as much as his beatings, and in fact, I would have probably chosen the silent beatings over her voice.

I think of how easily I could take him out. My foot fidgets at the thought. I lean to one side; it would just take one kick, a hard punch, there's not much left to him. He smells of cold cardboard, mildew; he is sour inside.

I lean down, take in his features: the gray eyebrows, the broad smile like my own, the arthritic hands, the stiff jawline, the disheveled yellow hair. The pulpit would have to hold him up now, not the other way around.

"Here, Pop, grab my arm. I'll pull you up." I put my hand out and stare up at the ceiling. His skin feels hot to the touch; he's heavier than I thought he would be. I am frozen inside.

When I've pulled him up all the way, we stare at each other, feel the gravity trying to pull us back down. I've not been this close to him in many years. We are the same height for the first time; neither of us looks away. We search the other for as far as we can go; we hold on, climb, wince, twist, and turn. It happens so fast. His eyes are wet, and when they pool over, I look away, blink, my skin burns.

Ma comes to the end of the hallway but doesn't say anything. The afternoon light reaches into the side window strong and hot; my skin prickles when I look at the oblong triangle we make in the hallway, the sharp edges we've always had, then the symmetry. It's not special; you can't tell that it is us.

I hand him his cane and walk out the front door and head north. The leaves move in the trees above me and the sky is dry. I feel paralyzed, can't tell if what I feel is pride, destruction, or the aftermath; there isn't a palpable beginning or end to it.

I keep walking, then start to run. I remember times when life was good, when the childhood memories were cherry in color and bled together, full and ripe, mouthfuls of them. The memories of those days used to flood me in Dallas at the weirdest times. Memories of when I'd watch cartoons on Saturday mornings, holding my mother's hand, while she smoked Salems and laughed at the television with me, the old TV set buzzing; or sitting atop my father's shoulders, fishing pole in hand, the low-hanging leaves of the trees brushing my head as we hiked down the trail to the Gulf in East Texas.

I run through the neighborhoods of Eton and feel as though gravity has left me behind, that I'm destined to float through space, or bump along, hitting things here and there forever, never finding solid ground. It's the way it's always been. Touch-and-go.

When I run long enough to get the high, I pay attention again, slip into the present. There is a sense of randomness in Eton, to the order of things here: houses and then trailers, white, white, white, and then an occasional black. The patterns here are hard to find, yet easy to identify. I count the number of houses I pass, the number of barefoot children, the curse words I hear; I see the dirty, old furniture on porches, skinny men on street corners, old cars on blocks in drives. Then the grandeur: the mountains so much softer and bluer than the Rockies, the sweet, melon air, the gusts of wind, the quiet calm of life here, the space in between it all.

*   *   *

A few days later, I am sitting at the kitchen table with Ma drinking a cup of coffee from one of the old plastic mugs we've used for years. The edges of the rim are frayed; the plastic chafes my lips as I drink.

"Carmine, your father, well, he's real sorry for how hard he was on you back when you were just a boy." She's drinking out of the same brown mug, and her hand shakes noticeably as she brings the cup to her mouth. She's got a lifetime worth of something she's holding back, and I'm always afraid the dam will break when I'm around.

I run my hands over my face, feel the stubble, the rawness of my own face. There hadn't been a day in twenty years that I haven't shaved, but there've been ten lately. I wake up and don't know what to do with myself anymore. My clothes are loose, they hang. My shirt is wrinkled and stained, I fold it at the elbows and go.

"You see, he didn't always know what was right, how to raise you good, you know? But you gotta know he meant well and that he loved you—you know that, right?" She lights another cigarette and stares at me with those same wet eyes.

I look back at her, don't blink or frown, just look back. I fold my legs beneath me and the table, fidget in my seat. I don't know what she's talking about.

"I hear you, Ma." I can hear the train passing in the distance; it rattles the house. The washing machine on the back porch switches cycles, a phone rings in the neighborhood somewhere; all of life is happening at once.

*   *   *

I wake up from a dream that night to hear my father scream: this is the worst that it has gotten, and I don't know how to let it pass without grabbing hold of it and trying to wrestle it to the ground. Give it a good fight. Make it go away.

"Lord, take me. Goddamn it—take me!" His cries are muffled by the sound of Ma pacing the wood floors, a scuffling sound, her feet pushing the energy from room to room. She stops at Dad's bedside again, and I can see the hunch of her old back in my mind, I hold my groin and listen. Wait. Hope she can do something to make it stop. Just make it fucking stop.

In Dallas everything, anything was within reach. I hold myself tighter and fall into another dream. I am commanding death, a cloaked figure, to come and take the old man away; a weary fog surrounds me. Whatever it costs, I'll pay it.

I chase the dream awhile, put the pillow over my head, manage to escape for an hour or two, less, more, I don't know. The heavy curtains are pulled in my room and there is nothing but black.

When I wake up again, my father is crying and screaming again, but the sounds are softer. Outside the heavy curtains, the dawn is busting through, and the light is a dull shade of pink.

"You son of a bitch, you motherfucker. I can't take this pain anymore . . ." My breathing is shallow as I listen and remember and feel small in this twin bed. I am suddenly aware of my own intestines, my liver, the beat of my heart pulsing warm blood through me. The bed squeaks beneath me as I turn.

In the morning, as I'm on my way out to the front porch for a smoke, Pa calls to me from his bedroom. His voice echoes off the paneling in the hall; so much of it comes back, the past is just a series of echoes bouncing off walls and I know it. I pause at his door for a second before stepping back into the hallway. I reach for something in my pocket; it's what I've always done: the silver money clip, loose change, even the cotton lining, something to stop the spin.

The house is quiet; Ma has stepped out for the morning. I am going out to fax some resumes. Two days ago, I left another message for Diego, hoping he'd have something in the works, hoping I could close my eyes and follow the next thing, sleep through another decade.

"Carmine, come in here for a second, would you?" When he speaks, he brings me back to this reality, but I am startled, and I don't know if I am in the present or remembering something again. His voice sounds old but still wicked and sour.

I walk into the room and smell him before I see him, find the footboard of the bed with my feet before I can see him; my eyes don't want to adjust to the light.

He clears his throat. I blink my eyes, and there he is.

"What's up?" I stop and look at him; he sags into the bed. I turn a pack of cigarettes and lighter in my hands, squeeze the end of the bed, hold back great images of attack, see planes fly around in my head and then crash-land.

"Listen, Carmine. Your ma, she's going to need you real soon. I've got nothing else to give her in this life, ain't had much to give her in a long time, if I ever did. I got nothing else to give nobody. Can't even get myself to the bathroom to take a shit anymore."

I look away, don't want to hear it, then look back at him. What does this have to do with me?

He's half the man he used to be, maybe less, his body slowly disintegrating. I feel like a king. I get bigger as he gets smaller, and it feels wicked good. I have nothing to compare him to anymore. His bulging biceps are now limp, his arms now wiry and sullen. He swims in his pajamas, and his echoing, billowing voice is now a whisper.

"Pop, Mom will be fine. I'll give her some money, look in on her sometimes. She's got friends, doesn't she? She'll be fine. I was just on my way out. Is that all?" I shake my head, punctuate my sentence with a long, deep breath, and leave the room. I light a cigarette before I reach the front door, wonder just where my legs will take me.

CHAPTER 8

THE NEXT AFTERNOON, I am laying on my bed, counting the ceiling tiles, the dust particles in the air. I hear my cell phone chime; there's a handful of voice messages I don't want to hear—Melanie, the landlord, the bank. I've been gone a month now, and I've not paid a thing, looked back at all; I am floating.

When it starts ringing, I jump out of bed, look at the handset, and realize it's Diego.

"Diego, my man, where ya been?" A smile climbs across my face, rises at the thought of being something again.

"Carmine, listen, I'm just calling out of real courtesy here, okay? There's nothing up. Nothing's happening, dude, and I'm serious about that." I hear his raspy voice on the other end of the line as he tells me that he's pretty much gone bankrupt and that he's run his business into the ground for years. I don't respond for a long time because I don't know what to say.

"I don't understand how that is possible, Diego. I mean, you built a fucking empire, and you're telling me that you don't have anything to stand on? Nothing at all? I find that hard to believe." I pound my hand on the small desk in my room, shake my head.

I want him to tell me it was all a joke, to come on home back to the high-rise, to my old life and my old office, and to get ready to fly again.

He doesn't. There is silence, except for the birds outside, the familiar hum of the old mail truck, Pa's cough a few doors down; there is actually nothing more happening.

He tells me a bunch of stuff about money and about deals gone bad and about angry clients and that he's moving back to Mexico to start from scratch again because he's totally connected there and knows he can make some quick money and live off his family for a while. Yeah, he says, it's not turned out like he thought it would be, but there's always something to chase, isn't there? Always another ride to jump on.

I hang up the phone and start laughing. It starts off slowly, my cheeks rising, a short, sharp hiccup from my chest, then I'm rolling, laughing so deep and hard that it hurts and I'm shaking. He's an old man, alone, a failure.

He's lived his whole life for nothing and he doesn't even know it.

*   *   *

The next morning I sleep in late and then jump out of bed and change my clothes, look at the pile of resumes on my old desk, the crisp white paper, curled at its edges now from humidity, the sharp ink of the laser printer from the printshop downtown. I leave them and walk out the door.

I try not to, but I think of that dead brown flesh often first thing in the morning, how I silently agreed with what was happening and how I've hated myself for it since. I can't be here in Eton, see old familiar faces, his kin, and not think of him and how Pa made it seem all right. Does this have to stay the same? Will it always look like this?

I head north toward that old church. The morning air is cool. I pick up my pace and feel the gravel of the street twist beneath my feet. In the hills behind me, I hear a rifle shoot; up the street, the long exhaustive sigh of a school bus.

Pa's cancer is getting stronger; it multiplies and he sleeps a lot now, and I've gotten used to his moans now. In the back of my mind it is muffled the same way Dallas traffic was, or the planes flying overhead from Dallas-Fort Worth; I hear it but I don't.

It might not be right, but I want to say good-bye to him after he's already gone, when he's just a thought, not a body, a slab of marble on a piece of dirt, a few forms I need to sign, a couple of details to take care of. I've been thinking about the mind full of things he'll die with, wonder if he longs for anything, wants a chance to do it over, or if he'll die the bastard he always was. Does a man keeping running long after the race is over, like Diego, or do some stop and look back?

Does he miss the old fish fries we used to have on Friday nights back in the old days in East Texas? Does he remember the smell of the corn batter, the Dixie music coming from someone's parked truck, the smell of wet fish on our clothes from work on the boats? But when I get my nerve up to cross the threshold of that bedroom door, to have a real conversation with him, an image of him, violent and unpredictable, comes running through my mind, pushes the backs of my legs, and I run again.

When I get close to the clapboard building, the sun is still low behind it, the sky a cornflower blue. I walk up the steps and open the door and smell the coffee brewing somewhere in the building; I can even smell the Styrofoam cups and the disinfectant on the floors and the Pledge on the pews. I hate the way it takes me right back, makes me small again, my brain just an organ with a memory, not my own to use.

The altar looks different today. The wooden cross seems bigger, yet less foreboding. Why would anyone want to stare at something so gruesome and call it life? Instead of going to the front, I sit in an empty pew at the back of the room and stare at the vaulted ceiling, run my hands across the glossy wood of the pew in front of me, listen for sounds around me.

Pa used to hold my hand as we walked from home to church every Sunday; his leathery skin felt like a big baseball glove holding mine' I remember looking up at his face, squinting in the sun, following his jawline, and hoping to make it right somehow, to read the secret map well enough to be able to find the meaning of the myth, the location of the real treasure he wanted me to find, to save myself.

I hear him mumbling prayers under his breath; his speech tired, he mumbles through it.

I watch each word take form in his mouth. The syllables are sweet and whole like a pregnant belly. He squeezes my hand, says, "say it with me, boy," and starts again. He wants to believe it. My mouth begins to move with his, I whisper, put one foot in front of the other, fill my chest with air and chant with him.

I don't hear the preacher walk up behind me, but when I turn around, I get the feeling that he's been there awhile.

"You came back." In the early morning light, his skin looks lighter, his black hair shinier. He reminds me of a cleaner version of George Jefferson, his voice much softer and calmer.

"Good morning. I know you said I needed to make an appointment, but the thing is, I just woke up this morning and walked out the front door and here I am."

He walks closer to me. I hear someone in the hallway to the left call his name.

"I'll be right there." He keeps his eyes on me, tender, tolerant. I feel a sense of panic within, but I stay seated in the pew.

"I've got to take care of a few things. If you'll wait awhile, I can sit down with you this morning." His eyes are a deep almond brown; he doesn't blink, but doesn't penetrate either—he is just there.

"All right, I will."

He turns and walks away. I see him disappear into the hallway, a mixture of voices fade, and then all is silent again.

I sit in the pew and close my eyes again, and after a few minutes, I am a boy again, about age ten. Ma sits beside me. I can smell the nicotine hanging on her bones. She reaches over and grabs my hand; I pull away. I don't trust her anymore.

She stands in the hallway and watches as Pa makes me read lines of scripture from the Bible until late into the night, until I can't keep my eyes open, until I'm crying and slobbering onto the brittle pages of the Book and Pa becomes angrier.

He pulls my head up by my hair and looks at me hard. "Start again, son, start again. Redeem yourself!"

I push back the tears, see Ma put her head down when I look at her out of the corner of my eye, lift my face, and breathe in deep. She leaves the threshold and goes back to her room; I hear the clink of her liquor bottle, and then the door closes.

Pa paces the kitchen and reads from his tattered Bible. "Listen, boy, listen to me," he tells me as he points to the book and recites over and over again.

Matthew 24:12-14: "Because of the increase of wickedness, the love of most will grow cold, but he who stands firm to the end will be saved. And this gospel will be preached in the whole world as a testimony to all nations, and then the end will come."

The kitchen light above our kitchen sink burns bright; I stare at it until everything turns black.

I think I fall asleep, because when Pastor Stanley comes back, for a second I think Pa is above me again. I sit inside myself with a handful of sins and wait.

CHAPTER 9

A FEW DAYS LATER I'm sitting in a café on Main Street eating a club sandwich looking at the want ads in the *Eton Gazette*. I think I could pour coffee here or load lumber at the old lumberyard or sell cars or mow lawns; it doesn't matter, I know. I think of reinventing myself, of taking a low profile, of disguising myself and starting all over.

I listen to the voices around me, hear the long, drawn-out drawl of the locals and how they're fixin' to do this and fixin' to do that. I put my head down and pretend not to notice. People know I'm not a complete stranger; they recognize something about me, but they look at me closely just the same: their eyes pierce me, take apart my clothes, try to count the dollars I have, if I get forty-dollar haircuts, if I'm just passing through or planning to stay awhile, wonder about the places I've been and the stuff I know. I feel them looking. I return the gaze, wonder the same things about them, if they want to put their feet on another part of the world, if they want to see what's around the mountain's edge, if they want to change things like bigotry and hatred and poverty, if they really love their lives or if they're just spending time. And then we both look away.

I stare out the window and watch the cars pull in and out of parking spots on the streets. The motions are so slow here; the cars back in and out like there's nothing in front or behind. I tap my foot under the table.

Across the street, I see Pa's old truck. The license plate hangs off the back, the muffler sputters loudly, but the motor is strong; there is no mistaking it. I am surprised to see them, both of them out of the house at the same time. I didn't know Pa could do it, that they could manage. I've been sleepwalking. I don't know what goes on.

I pick up a wedge of sandwich and watch my mother pull into a parking spot in front of the doctor's complex across the street; the big white steering wheel makes a circle, and then she straightens the wheels and turns the truck off. Just like that.

I am a stranger watching a scene from a movie. I chew on a piece of bread, pick up a French fry, watch. A kid puts a quarter in the old jukebox near the door, and Randy Travis starts singing. This can't all be backdrop.

Someone walks up to the truck, and I can see Ma's mouth moving. Her long fingers pointed down the street at something; then I see her looking down and messing with something in her lap. In the front seat, Pa's head sags to the right and he leans on the doorjamb; I am not sure if he's actually still in that body. His long arm hangs out the door, his fingers slide across the faded paint of the door. He always loved that old truck. I remember him washing and waxing it every weekend, shining the interior, even hosing the engine. He even kept driving it after the ignition failed and he had to start it with a screwdriver. I can't believe it is still around.

I watch my parents, hear the clang of dishes and silverware in the diner, take a long drink of my Coke and rattle the ice around in the cup. How is it that I'm in this place at this time with this window?

I see Ma walk around the truck to Pa's side and open his door. He holds his body in and waits; he's wearing a button-down sweater with his pajama bottoms. Ma's hair is pulled back into a ponytail, but strands of it stick to her face as she struggles to get him out and standing.

My feet won't move me, even though I see Ma's purse fall to the ground as Pa steps out of the truck and his weight leans on her. My feet still don't move when I see Ma wedge Pa up against the truck as she opens the tailgate and pulls out the old wheelchair and pushes him into it.

*   *   *

Later that afternoon, I'm walking around town, making big circles around the tavern but not going in. The next thing I know, I'm at that old clapboard church again, staring into the dark eyes of the pastor. I can't seem to stay away.

"The thing is, pastor, I just don't know what any of it means. I don't know if it means anything, this life, this earth, family, careers, how we spend our time, or if it all means nothing, if it's just empty space, if I need to worry more about living or dying." I put my head in my hands and run my fingers through my hair. I pick up the glass of water on the table and take a small drink. It's warm, like the air.

He sits across from me in the old meeting room of the church, his hands folded, one leg over the other. I remember this room. We used to have Sunday school in here. Sometimes Pa held Bible study; other times he used it to store some of the furniture he was hoping to sell to the church members.

The room is square, walls covered in dull floral wallpaper, brown, the corners of it peeling. I think it was always like this. The big window in the room lets in so much light, it's almost overpowering; you've got to squint unless the shades are drawn.

I tell him about my whole life. My youth. My career. My money. All my nice things. The chaise in Dallas and the women and all the alcohol I've consumed and that I'm a mean person. I tell him about Pa, how he sat in this very room, a bigoted hypocrite, how I promised myself I'd be better than him. How I followed in Diego's footsteps but don't want to be like him either. I start to tell him how I watched a boy be killed without helping him, but it's too much. I stop, look away.

"Carmine, success and power are relative terms. They can mean many things to many people. Your ideas of success and power and material things have come to mean many things to you. For you, these things have become your life, define you as a man. But there's more to the story, and we can change the details anytime.

"For a lot of people, success often becomes a drug, or another form of alcohol, a means to escape something they feel is chasing them, something they don't want to feel. We also seek influence, fame, or success as a means to give us purpose and make us feel valuable. Then when we do something wrong, fail ourselves or others, we live by that guilt. It's the wrong way to do it."

"Yes, pastor, I get what you're saying, but if life is not these things—being mean or climbing or whatever—what is it? I mean, what actually matters?" I can feel myself start to sweat behind my ears; my heart beats faster. I want to know something. Somewhere in the distance a clock ticks loudly. I tap my feet, listen.

"Ultimately, the meaning of life is not found in how we've defined ourselves or what we've done. Those things are just extensions of the things we believe. The meaning of life, the real crux of our existence, is found solely in our relationships. When the relationships are meaningful, then success, power, influence, a cause, life, death, a legacy, and sacrifice for others all become meaningful and purposeful."

He tells me a little more about scripture and what it says about success and power and how man was made, but I don't hear him. I want to ask him what you do when you have no relationships at all, but I don't.

I leave the church, and for the rest of the day, I walk. Search. Make an effort to connect dots, find meaning in the space between this thing and that, the soil beneath my feet, the women I've been in bed with, the parents I've hated, the deals I've shaken, the last time I felt anything close to love.

I walk until my legs feel weak and I come around the corner of our street. The long leaves of the sidewalk trees lean down and touch the top of my head; the locusts scream. I see the old blue truck parked in the drive.

*   *   *

"Carmine? You there?" I'm stepping out of the shower when I hear Pa's voice down the hall. I freeze.

"Carmine? If you're there, please come . . ."

I can barely hear him, and his voice trails off until it disappears completely. Panic comes over me; it feels like electricity in my bones. The bathroom mirror is foggy, and I use my forearm to clean it off. I stare at myself in the foggy mirror and wait to know what to do next, wait to feel the next instinct point me in a direction. Nothing happens. The house is so quiet, still; my hair drips down my face.

I put a towel around my waist and lean out of the bathroom door.

"Ma? Ma, you home?" The hair is cold and I feel goose bumps on my skin. I close the bathroom door and wait, towel still around my waist. I sit down on the stool and tap my foot.

I look up after a few minutes, and the fog has cleared from the mirror. I get a good look at myself then, notice the crow's feet stretching around my eyes, a few gray hairs at my temples.

The house is still so quiet, except for the passing of the train in the distance, a delivery truck on the street.

I put on my jeans and T-shirt and step out in the hallway slowly. There is no sound coming from Pa's room, not even the squeak of the bedsprings or his cough. I feel afraid. I'm not ready to deal with this, I think, as I walk slowly down the hall toward my parents' room.

I stand at the doorway quietly and wait. The room is filled with the white noontime light. I see him laying on the bed, motionless, and I can't tell if he's alive or dead. A few thoughts pass through. First, a sense of euphoria, a real glee in the seat of my pants, then utter terror, as though I'm spiraling in outer space without the cord that holds me to the ship. It all happens so fast.

I walk closer to the bed, and then I see him breathing, but his chest barely swells, barely raises the blanket he's covered with.

"Pa? Pa, you awake?" I touch his arm and his eyes pop open.

"Carmine, Carmine, son, I can't breathe . . . I can't breathe." I see a single tear roll down his cheek and his hand reaches for me, tries to grip my arm. I pull away. He gasps for air.

I stand there looking at him. His lips move again but no sound comes out, except dry, throaty air. It sounds like something being dragged across a concrete floor.

"You can't breathe, Pa, is that what you said?" My stomach flips.

He nods his head. I see beads of sweat forming on his brow. I look around the room just then, notice that it looks much the same as it did when I was a boy. There is a layer of dust on everything, and Ma and Pa's old wedding photo still sits on their dresser.

I look back at Pa again. He stares at me and breathes so softly I can barely hear him wheeze. He searches my face like I once did his.

"I don't want to watch you die, old man." I pull the covers up close to his chin. I can't feel him breathe beneath my hands.

His eyes close for a while, his palms unfold, he seems to relax, to give up something inside. The color begins to leave his face, and he seems to sink into the bed.

"I don't know what I'm supposed to do here," I say to the room. An old song comes back to me—"we all got blues." I feel so mad all of a sudden, like I could burst right out of my skin, paddling my chest. Pastor Stanley is wrong. Why would anyone actually want to love someone when it comes to this?

"Boy, I don't want to die . . ."

He's crying now, so softly, like a boy; his face looks like a version of myself. I feel my heart beat faster in my chest; my legs grow weak. I lock my knees and stand up straighter.

"What's it like, Pa? To be in this place? In this room like this?" I pull a chair up to the bed and sit. He doesn't have enough breath to answer me.

He shakes his head, stops crying, stares at me.

"I watched someone die once, and I've never forgiven myself. But this is different. It's time we have a talk, don't you think?" I pull the chair closer and pat the edge of the bed.

"Did it make you feel better to hurt me? To tear me down? I hear that people hurt others because they hurt; that the hurt had to start somewhere, otherwise it wouldn't be. Do you believe this, Pa?" I look at him and wait for an answer.

His eyes pool, but he doesn't say anything, saves his breath and keeps looking at me.

I am up on my feet now. I circle the room and pace, run my hands through my wet hair.

"Old man, I've been wanting to repay you all of these years. I've been wanting to see you suffer; my whole life I've waited to have you on your back." My fists clench and I move my feet back and forth, rock in place. I am afraid of what I might do, if there is something evil that still resides within me, if it ever did.

The sun reaches into the window above their bed and casts a shadow of myself on the floor in front of me, tall and lean. I am small and big at the top, monstrous. My feet are as firm as they've always been. I can do what I want with this moment; it stands in front of me, the past finally immobile.

I stand at the front of the room and watch the dust particles float in the air, smell the hint of sleep and sickness in the room, the particular sweetness of my folks, the way it's always been, the way things are. I get lost in the moment for a few seconds.

My fists relax; my heels rest on the floor. I remember Stanley again, his round head, the way he rests his hands on the end of his knees when he talks to me.

"If a man has a son of a bitch as a father, is that all he's destined to be, Pa?"

His face is completely white now, his forehead covered in sweat. His eyes are so wet I can see through them, to the back of his head. I see nothing that I thought was there.

Pa shakes his head, pushing the weight of it from side to side the best he can. He takes all his strength to push his head up, reaches for my hand again. I pull away. We sit together, both of us looking off into some lone place. We stay like this for a few seconds, maybe minutes or hours, I don't know.

CHAPTER 10

WHEN MA CAME HOME that afternoon, she nearly fainted when I told her the ambulance had just left with him, that he'd turned white from lack of oxygen and couldn't speak. I watched the red ambulance lights leave the house and travel through town from the end of the street.

"He's fine, Ma, he's fine."

She falls into me, and I hear her rattled breathing on my chest.

"We had a little talk and I called 911." I pull away from her and look at her as I speak.

She sits down on the sofa and sighs deeply. I go to the kitchen to get her a cup of coffee; the old percolator is lukewarm.

"Was he afraid, Carmine? I only left for just an hour." She searches my face.

"He was," I tell her, and I think about the terror he must have felt as I paced the room as he gasped for air.

"He shouldn't be alone. I have to go to him." Ma fidgets, twists her hands, and shakes as she drinks her coffee.

"You should," I say.

"Won't you come with me?"

*   *   *

There is nothing original about the Crazy Horse Bar or the fact that we've stumbled in there. I am beginning to think that life is not as chaotic as we think, that there may be real order to things. A series of ins and out, yeses and nos; is it possible that life is just what we pay attention to? Or is it the same scene run over and over again, back-to-back, like a reel from a black-and-white movie that has malfunctioned and keeps circling and circling.

The reputation of this place precedes it. People talk. Around town, people call it the Shack. It is a hole-in-the-wall, a dive, but inside, there are the most beautiful women in Atlanta, pretty and soft; they don't know what they could do. It is a sad sort of irony, makes me think of the way bunnies are eaten by coyotes and newborn babies are born with their mothers' habits, before they have a chance to become themselves.

The building has a lean to it; it nearly dips down to the ground and back up again. The metal siding gleams in the moonlight, threatening, piercing. The night is chilly and again it is wet. When we get out of the car—me, Mark, and Griff—I shake my head, think about Ma alone at the hospital. Why have I come back here and with them?

I've been so many places lately: on window ledges, in my old bed, at the church, by Pa's side. The phone still never rings and I still can't see any shapes in my future, don't know where I'll go, what I'll do; I grasp at images hoping to find the outline of something solid.

Mark and Griff had shown up at my door, loud, obnoxious; they think they know me, and I am not sure if they do or don't. They said we should drive to Buckhead, throw a few back, talk about old times, remember how things used to be, cut up, they said. I told them Pa's just been taken to the hospital, that he's dying for real, that Ma's on the way there. I said, "Let's jump in the car and get out of here."

We walk up the sidewalk. It is ten o'clock. Nothing is happening, but people are flowing into the building; and when the door opens, the music pours out and I can feel it in my legs. The lights above the dance floor bounce on and off the walls. There are women with trays walking around, young people. I try to remember myself here as a teenager, sneaking in with fake IDs and big plans; I always knew what I wanted to take from life.

The place is packed: southern belles trying to look otherwise, college kids, a flow of women swarming back and forth in tight clothes and ideas, tall guys waiting for a chance to move in, to be someone.

I remember the women in Dallas, the ones I canvassed here in my youth. My tongue wanders the walls of my mouth; it's a reflex, but I wouldn't mind doing it all over again.

There were a few places I frequented in Dallas, places where my drink and name were known, places where my reputation preceded me and I felt welcome, at least as the Carmine that I was, predictable, rotten at the edges, but charming and light on his feet; it was always such an easy dance. The Opium Den was one of them. It comes alive in my mind, even while sitting in the Shack, the memories of its dark and elegant corridors and private party rooms, the dark shade of lighting, the way you could disappear within it.

The club sounds like an adult wonderland, rides and tonics, sex and drugs, a roller coaster I've been on too many times to count. There are lines of people waiting to get on, and they are sweaty and hot and irritated; and instead of limp paper tickets in their hands, they hold sweaty dollar bills, the cover charge, the price they'll pay to be someone else for the night.

The Saturday-night crowd is full of energy. I watch them as though for the first time. Who are they?

There are bodies lined along the wall like slabs of meat, bloody and cold. I feel as anesthetized as a butcher; I am in the same room for the same reasons, but we are not the same.

It's the perfect environment for forgetfulness. Separation fills the room; everyone is absent. Then—the dance. Back and forth, swaying, waiting to touch, to become bigger than what we are. I know it, but do they?

The three of us sit around a table, and I order a shot of whiskey. It burns going down my throat but feels good, familiar, first the shock and then the burn; finally the glow comes, soft and gentle.

"You ain't been out in weeks, bro. What's up?" Griff is wearing a baseball cap and a Pink Floyd T-shirt. He drinks a draft beer in two gulps.

"You know how it is," I say, smiling; don't know what else to say. I eat from the bowl of peanuts on the table, down another shot; the nuts feel salty in my mouth, the whiskey hot.

"Well, it ain't never as bad as it seems," Mark says, taking a drink of his Coke.

"Is your old man at home dying?" I ask him, scanning the room, then resting my eyes heavily on him.

"Aw, come on, let's loosen up and have some fun." Griff laughs and stands up, comes around and starts rubbing my shoulders. "Just look at all these opportunities."

I look around, can't make out anything specific anymore, just blurred images, swatches of color, forms moving up and down. Mark and Griff start making animal sounds, slapping their bellies, pointing at people in the crowd. I push my chair back from the table to get a good look at them. So little has changed about them; minds and bodies are the same, they tread all the same dirt. We cannot be from the same past, I think.

There's a center stage in the bar, wood, raised above the dance floor by half a foot, scuff marks all over it; it's been there a while. A waitress has just completed a number, and the music fades behind her. I feel like I've been here, in this moment before. I think I hear running water somewhere, an odd echo; something is passing above me.

The crowd cheers but I stay silent, taste the salt still left in my mouth, feel the whiskey in my veins, the blood starting to go to my cock, I bite my lip.

I pick up a menu to order food, but it only has songs in it. I put it down. I feel hot, sweaty. Mark and Griff continue to talk loudly, the room buzzing louder. I consider what else I could be doing.

"What's this?" The menu is full of songs, old ones, CCR, new ones too, others.

"You get to pick a song, and for ten bucks they'll send one of the girls to do the number," Mark says as he scans the room.

"Get a fast song. I want to see everything move." Griff laughs as I decide on Melissa Ethridge's "Bring Me Some Water." I don't know why I've chosen this one or if I've heard it before, but I like how the title sounds. I raise the menu into the air to get someone's attention.

A tall black woman walks to the table so quietly she's barely noticed by anyone. She's beautiful in a way that puts you in awe of the human race, just like newborn babies and giant oak trees and talking cars. Who knew it was possible? She's in her late twenties, tall and eloquent. Her face has that grown-up look, the small lines around her eyes like sculpture, the fullness in her cheeks; her body is round and soft everywhere. Her hair is braided, and her eyes stare out in the shape of almonds, perfectly oval. I have never looked at anything so closely.

"Which one of you boys picked the hardest song on the menu?" she asks, not even looking at me as I point to the song on the menu.

"If you don't know the song, then have them send someone who does." Griff takes a big drink of his draft beer, looks around the room again, and scratches himself.

"I know the song." She looks at him intently as she says it, as though she has something to prove, her hip sticking out slightly, her eyes barely glance at me.

"Look! Here's $10; we'll pay you, and you don't have to sing." I watch them talk, but I don't say anything. I can hear glass clink on tables and platform shoes slide across the dance floor; there's a DJ in the corner of the room.

"I work for my money. I'll do the song. See those girls over there," she says, and points to a group of rowdy bleached-hair, big-bosomed women on the dance floor. "They like fun guys. I know them well; they're here all the time. If you guys holler and act like I'm the best thing you've seen in a long time, they'll be all over you before this song is done. So don't do it for me; do it for mankind."

She picks up the mic on the tray and looks around the room sadly. This is not where she wants to be either.

"What's your name, baby?" she asks, finally looking at me.

I am intimidated by her, her black skin, the unfamiliarity of her voice; I don't know what these new feelings mean. I am simultaneously repulsed and turned on. I feel the old sourness that has been at the bottom of my gut for years. My groin reacts, and I shift my weight to try to move the blood.

She begins to sing and leans over me, her long braids touching the sides of my face; my insides tremble, I am a shell of a man these days. I feel her sing from inside, know she's known great sorrow in her life, that her insides twist and turn, too, that she knows the bloody fight for forgiveness.

When will this aching pass

When will this night be through

I want to hear the breaking glass

I only feel the steel of the red hot truth . . .

In the periphery, I see the guys and hear her sing; she floats around the room and I'm somewhere above it.

"Carmine? Carmine? Are you with us, bro?" Mark laughs.

"You see me sitting here, don't you?" I push my empty shot glass away from me.

"Why do you keep looking at that black broad?" he yells over the music.

"Shut the fuck up, Griffin. Just shut up."

She continues to sing. When she's done, she laughs as she collects all the money that's been thrown on her tray, stuffs it into her apron pocket, and puts her empty tray on the bar.

When she's done talking to someone and leaning up against the bar, I walk up to her, stretch out my hand as if at a business meeting; it hangs in the air, and I feel stupid. I am fifteen again and she is a senior. I put my hands in my pockets.

"Hey—that was amazing," I say to her back as she's walking away.

She hurries away through the side door of the bar, an emergency exit with no alarm. I stand there, follow the curves in her back, wait, somehow expect her to turn around and come back—they always do.

I sit down again. The song stays in my head for a long time. I get a bottle of water from the bar, sit back down, look at Griff and Mark and the black boy in the back of my head. My ears begin to ring.

I tell them I'm ready to go, and I begin to walk toward the front of the bar, looking for the entrance; the room spins and my eyes are blurred. Someone is up on the stage singing, but it's not her. The lights circle in rainbows, and the sensations land in various places within my body, but none of it feels right. I feel sick.

"Carmine, wait up. I've got some business to handle here before I go."

I turn around. Griff is holding a round girl on his lap, and his face is buried in her chest; she laughs with one hand in the air moving to the music and takes long and slow drags off a cigarette with the other. Mark is whispering in the ear of another girl. They both have wives at home.

I sit at an empty stool at the end of the bar to gain my balance and wait. I watch the crowd some more, but don't see a sign of her—or any other black person, I now notice. I feel hot and cold at the same time, remember Pa gasping for air, feel moments away from screams of my own.

I look for her one last time before I pull my body from the stool and walk outside into the night air, find the bumper of Griff's old car.

Later, when we are driving back home to Eton, I let whatever's been knocking take me over completely.

CHAPTER II

I COME OUT OF my room in the middle of the night to use the bathroom and hear Ma in the living room. Pa is still at the hospital. The house is eerily quiet.

"Carmine, baby, sit down." She hasn't called me baby in a long time; the memory of her using it at all is so distant, I think it must be the memory of someone else's mother I am remembering, not my own.

"I'm real tired, Mom, real tired." I sit down on the corner of the brown couch and wait while my eyes try to find focus.

It is three in the morning and I'm still buzzed. She is drinking cold coffee from that old brown mug; she always liked it that way. Her breathing is so shallow I wonder how it supports any thoughts at all, emotions; any second she'll spill right out of there.

"You know, Carmine, I loved you as best I could; your pa too. We ain't perfect, we never was, but that don't matter as much as you think."

I can see her now. Her arms and legs are bony-thin; her voice is soft. Parts of her hair are still golden like a little girl's. I twist and turn at my end of the couch, think about how she used to be. Supple, happy. It was back when she'd first started drinking, back when it'd been fun, when we'd sometimes go fishing at nine o'clock on a school night late into the night.

I remember the fullness of her lovely arms around my small neck, tucking the overgrown hair behind my ears, lifting me up and tucking me in and swallowing me whole.

"We'll be burying that old man soon, and some things need to be said around here before that happens. You've been gone so long, boy, so long, and I've been wanting to make it right for a long time. The only right I know, the only right I got." She pulls another menthol from the side pocket of her house jacket, but she waits to light it.

I study her face; I try not to, but I can't help it. Her skin sags; the bones in her cheeks are so prominent, and her eyes so blue—the bluest I've ever seen—and so wet. Her skin is pale, so white; she never had a lot of color. Her hair hangs soft and light, and even the gray can't compete with its golden color. Has she always looked like this?

My mouth is dry; I bleed into the couch. I try so hard to remember another woman I've loved. There is no one.

"What do you want from me, Ma?" My voice is cracked at the edges, but not rough. I turn my face toward her, lean to one side, then straighten and rest my elbows on my knees.

I hear her blow the smoke out of her lungs and see her cross her ankles.

"I want my peace, boy, peace, the same as everyone else."

"Peace? What is that?" I say it snidely, as though she won't know the answer to it. I cross my leg over my knee, make a number four, lean my head back.

"It's when you ain't mad no more." She holds me to each word, her eyes never looking away. Outside an owl hoots as if in support.

I look at her for a long time, and a bunch of images pass behind my eyes. Old girlfriends, the time I got mugged in the street, the lunch line in middle school—what does one thing have to do with another?

For the first time in years, I recognize a feeling: I am hungry, famished. The feeling is so strong.

"Ma, let's eat. Do you want to eat something with me?" I stand up; I feel frantic.

She stubs her cigarette out in the ashtray on the end table, stands up beside me. "Yes, son, I'd like that. I'd like that a lot."

An hour later, we sit in front of a feast. We drink thick chocolate milk and eat cheesy grits and bologna, some leftover potato salad, big dill pickles, Ritz crackers. The kitchen light is dull, and the house seems strange without Pa's labored coughing.

We sit at that old Formica table and gorge ourselves for close to an hour without talking. I eat until my stomach is bulging, my throat wet, my body so tired and full. When we're done we lean back in our chairs and look at each other across the table, over the scraps of what's left—a half roll of crackers, the crusty bottom of the grits pan, the empty yellow bologna package. The brown Formica is chipped but still shines in the night light.

"Thanks, Ma," I tell her as I shuffle out of the room. I walk slowly to my room and fall back into bed, feeling like my mother's son, a swaying, salty sleep, the smell of water all around me. I suppose men, even myself, are perpetually boys. The sons of parents who provide the staples of what makes up a life—a home, an example of what it means to be human, however fucked up that may be. We are molded by impressions and an example, single days that stick out, and wounds that split us open and never close. We take on other people's pain and sometimes make them ours.

*   *   *

The day the hospital tells us Pa is better off at home, that there's not much to be done at this point, that the machine will help him breathe and we should make things as easy as possible for him, we sign a pink piece of paper and take him home. It takes more to sign a marketing deal, I think, than it does to deliver news like this.

My mind drifts to other things late that night. I can't get that girl off my mind, the Buckhead T-shirt she was wearing and the smart smile, her long legs, the energy circulating around her, even the way she walked away from me.

I toss and turn in the twin bed and think of her again. The left side of my brain tries to remind me of blondes and blue eyes, but the right, the soft and tender cerebellum of mine, remembers every detail about her, the mixture of lust and confusion I felt.

I can hear Ma out in the kitchen, smell the cigarette smoke lingering in the morning, feel the living room light pushing in under my door. It's a weird feeling, preparing for death, an ending. The hospice nurse tells Ma and me it's our job to keep him comfortable, but I am not sure what exactly that means.

I pull on some clothes and step out of my room. I pass Pa's room and hear him cough, feel the vibration of his oxygen machine, keep going, head toward the coffeepot in the kitchen.

"How he's doing, Ma?"

She's sitting at the table sewing some buttons on one of Pa's pajama shirts; she runs her hand up and down its crease as she goes.

I pull up a chair beside her and sip my coffee slowly. It's barely past six in the morning; I've only been asleep a few hours.

"I don't know. I don't know. Your pa, he's a fighter and he ain't done fighting yet, but I don't think it will be much longer. He knows he can't win this one. He don't even really want to." She cuts the thread and ties the final knot before folding the shirt up and moving on to another, a baby blue one, thin from laundry; it's been pressed and starched.

"He always did like a good fight, didn't he?" I take another sip of my coffee and look at her softly, my eyes turned in. "You know what I mean, Ma."

She stops sewing for a minute and looks at me, like she's looking directly at my bones, past me, deeper and at something she doesn't know much about anymore but is familiar still, pulling, like a tree knows its own branches.

"Yeah, I know what you mean." She gets up and refills both our cups and tells me that hospice has put him on morphine and that he'll probably sleep more and more and that there are other things to expect, like confusion and dementia and emotional effects; it might be different every day.

"If you've got anything to say to your old pa, you'd better say it soon, son." She folds the last shirt and gets up from the table.

I'm listening, trying to connect with her words, but they all seem to be disconnected, just things people say at times like this.

"I'm real glad you're here, Carmine; we need to be together. We need to remember the good." She pushes her thick hand across the table to me and rests it on top of my own. I feel the calluses on her fingertips, remember them on my back as she washed me in the tub, the way she used to pull my tube socks up way high and hold my hand as we crossed the street.

"Yeah," I say, leaning my head to one side, squinting my eyes but meeting hers. I rinse my cup and then head out the front door again.

*   *   *

I walk and walk, end up in corners of town I've never seen, stare in shop windows full of antiques, a bakery selling nothing but cupcakes, a kids' dance school. My legs feel hot and I try not to think much, but something about the morning air, the golden sun peeking through the sky, makes me remember being in the fifth grade, gangly and

hot, gentle and kind. It's the special thing all kids have—
until life squashes it.

The end of the year had come around, and the school was
holding its annual science fair. I had built a volcano out of
hobby-store clay and inside had mixed together something
lethal enough to get smoke to rise up its crooked sides. I
spent hours on it in the kitchen each night, and I could feel
Ma's and Pa's soft eyes on me, gentle and approving, quiet
for once.

I remember that on this day, I thought of nothing but
that brown clay in my hands, the anticipation of getting
that smoke to billow out for me, the thought that Pa might
want to help, that life could be something other than Jesus
and guilt and fighting for redemption.

That volcano, as I birthed it, sat on the kitchen table
for weeks. We ate dinner around it, our plates hitting the
outside edges of the cardboard it sat on. I thought of it when
I went to sleep at night; it was the first thing I went to in the
morning, it was my creation, something completely within
my control, and I felt connected to it. I finally had some
power in the world.

My mind will only allow me to remember bits and pieces
of the rest, mostly because I don't want to: Pa drunk, me
falling asleep at the kitchen table, Ma crying in the living

room, a hump of clay on the floor, so many nights ending up in rotten fights.

When my eyes opened the next morning, I thought of the hump of clay on the floor and about how Pa never loved anything or cared about anything but Jesus and how I never knew how he was gonna get us to heaven that way.

When I got to the kitchen that morning, my volcano sat almost exactly as I'd molded it, except at the edges, along its slopes, were Pa's fingerprints, crooked but smooth and wide. Ma was in the living room chair smoking, quiet, but I could see her looking my way out of the corner of her eye.

"Ma, Pa fixed my volcano, do you see it? Ma, my volcano is right there. I get to go to the fair."

She nodded to me from the dark living room and smiled.

I carried that volcano, on its precarious cardboard foundation, all the way to school that day. The morning was cool and damp, and the sun squeezed itself through the tall pines in Eton and I felt proud, the mountains in the distance hovering over me protectively. My chest swelled and my pride knocked the chill out of the air, and it was enough to have this one thing.

Later that afternoon, the science fair opened, and awards were announced; my belly was full, I didn't want anything more. But here's the thing: I won that science fair—the whole big thing. When they announced my name, hands began to clap loudly from the group of parents standing in the corner of my school's gymnasium. I wasn't expecting it, but I recognized those hands.

When I stood up, I caught my first glimpse of Pa, his hands stretched above him, clapping, watching my volcano as it was wheeled to the front of the room. He looked around the room for me, but I stayed still, looking down at the tops of my shoes. I was so afraid of moving, of jolting the moment out of its place in time. He came up, stood next to me, behind that volcano, his hand on my shoulder, and while the cameras flashed and the applause continued, he looked at me and said, "You did good, Carmine, real good."

We stood in front of the volcano while the ribbon was placed on me, and I can still remember the heat of Pa's hand on my shoulder, the sound of the applause, even the feel of that cold clay.

* * *

When I make it to good old Preacher Stanley again, I can't help but smile like I'm that good boy again. I take a Styrofoam cup from the lobby, fill it up with coffee, head down the hall to his office, and sit down and wait. I've got a lot of work to do.

Chapter 12

THE DRIVE FROM ETON to Atlanta is for the most part uneventful, but the road rises and falls to meet you and there's a softness to the hills; they change from green to blue to orange and then there are trees and pavement and billboards and all the stuff you see most anywhere, somehow bright and natural and terrible all at the same time.

I am driving the old pickup truck, and I have to open my arms wide to grip the big white steering wheel, just like Ma does. I can see her fingerprints at the edges, small and pointed; her grip is stronger than I thought.

I hear its roar and feel its uncomfortable vibration, smell the dusty vinyl and remember riding to school in this thing. Sometimes after school Pa'd take me to deliver a piece of furniture, we'd pick up a cold Coke at a diner, and sit for a while. Times like these he'd say nothing, look in the distance beyond me; I wondered where and who he was. Pretty soon he'd come back to the Bible and that was the end of it; the space between us had to change.

The engine drags on and the wing window that won't close all the way whistles to me as I drive. I'm already imagining the ill-placement of this woman on that dirty stage, how she'll be smiling but how the backs of her eyes will probably be crying the way they were the other night, a reflection. I wonder if I can tell her anything she doesn't already know.

My focus is singular at this point, even if it is not completely clear: I just have to know her. If I can get her name tonight, if I can get her to speak to me without a songbook in her hand, I know we can go from there.

I drive, and I think. I remember my talk with Pastor Stanley.

"When we choose to forgive, we choose to lay aside our right to extract our revenge. In the moment of making that decision, we choose God, we choose peace, and the path of forgiveness is shown to us."

He stood up and grabbed a stone mug off the table and sipped it, one leg over the other; he smiled at me gently, like he always does. Down the hall, I heard the pans bang and the women talk. "When we take this step and try to forgive someone, we begin to find reasons for our hearts to turn toward mercy instead of malice."

I held very still and watched his soft pink lips move. I've been running and gunning my whole life, the world full of monsters; I have never thought about more than the woman or the buck in front of me. I don't know if I can see Pa as just a man with a pulse, an old guy with cancer, much less myself.

"The problem with forgiveness, you see, is not being able to forgive ourselves. When we choose not to forgive ourselves, the consequence is a destructive and hateful path. It's that simple."

At the Shack, the parking lot is full, but I somehow know she's folded in the walls of the building, I feel it so clearly, in the nerves of my arms and legs, in the buzz in my head. *What am I doing here? I've never chased a woman—and a black one at that!* I sit for another long minute before going in.

The club is as it was before, unrestrained and vacant, full of lights and colors and agendas. I find a table in the corner, near the stage, and wait. I order a plain Coke and search the room for her, imagine what I'll say, what I am really feeling, remember how I've picked up every other woman in my life, and wonder if any of it is important. Will she feel the old hate in my bones? Know that even though I've never even befriended a black person that I somehow know we have something to offer each other?

When she comes out from behind the stage, I am startled by the tenderness I feel within me; uncomfortable with it, I look away from her just as it seems she might be recognizing me. She introduces herself as Z, and her eyes gloss over, as though she's somewhere else. I don't want to, but I wave the waitress down and order a shot of tequila. It feels smooth sliding down the back of my throat, and when I look at her through the cloud of smoke in the room, I feel better, my upper hand assuring me that she can't hurt me.

The rest of the evening comes easier to me. I drink a lot, feel my old suit hanging on my old bones, watch her and pretend she is a work of art I might want to buy, an investment. I study her colors and the depth of her lines; I work the room.

"Why do you come here?" I ask the light-haired girl with long, full legs and small ears sitting next to me. She leans across the table toward me; I can feel her need to conquer me.

Out of the corner of my eye, I can see Z's braids sliding across her breasts, the twist of curl at the ends, her arms strong as she carries a tray of drinks to a table.

"I don't know; I guess the same reason everyone else does, to have fun." She looks around the room vacantly; her eyes are so blue and so young, and without imagining it, I think about taking her home, remember the nurse from a few weeks ago.

"Why do *you* come here?" she asks as she gets up, now on her feet, moving her hips back and forth to the DJ's drum. I smile and look at her for a long time before I answer her because she thinks she has me, and in a way she does, the old skin enveloping me, but sliding off, the way a snake gets rid of its scales.

"I'm looking for someone." I head to the bar to sober up and figure out how to approach Z without sounding too heavy or too light or as though I have an agenda, some making-up to do, or like the man I've always been and the hundreds she sees each night.

The girl heads to the dance floor and finds a set of arms to climb into. I order another drink and chew on the ice slowly.

For the last hour of the night, I sit and wait and watch her. I let my mind wander away at times and think of my mother at home or about odd career paths like becoming a race car driver or what squash blossoms taste like and if I could actually change the oil in the old truck.

When the music stops and the white lights come on, giving everyone a tired glow, I know I'll need to make a move before the bouncer is throwing me out and I have to drive the long road home to Eton without a single connection to her.

I get up from the bar and find her in the corner of the room, wiping a round table, her wood tray tucked under her arm. She breathes audibly as she pushes the towel in circles on the top of the table. Her skin is buttery and her clothes hug her, but I try not to think of her in only these terms.

"Can I help you?" she says, her body defensive, her voice direct and wiry. But her gaze softens, her eyes squint in the light, and she recognizes me.

I don't know what to say. I sit there looking at her.

"Are you lost?" She's gone hard again. I search her face for its origin, the pain that has chafed her insides and the fire that has fringed her edges. She turns around and starts wiping the table again.

"I'm Carmine."

She doesn't turn around, but I know she's listening by the curve of her back.

"I'm Z and I'm outta here." She laughs quietly and walks away from me, shaking her head, and I feel a vein of anger rise up within me. I let it pass and then I follow her.

"Listen, I'd like to have a cup of coffee with you or take a walk or sit with you a while. Can we do that?"

I shove my hands deeper in my pockets and try to find that old confidence, my old command of women, but I feel weak within, my parents' child, and I can't do anything but be there, the man with no job and the dying father, the one without a clue.

"Guy, I appreciate the offer, but I don't go out with men that come in here. Okay?" She removes the dirty glasses from her tray, two at a time, and sets them on the bar, then wipes her hands on the towel hanging from the apron around her waist.

"Thanks but no thanks is what I mean." She walks to the other end of the bar, where the cash register sits, and takes out the wad of bills from her apron pocket.

I feel confronted and excited all of a sudden, lost in some wilderness that is not my own, searching the sky for the right direction. I remember going hunting in the green hills with a group of good ol' boys in Dallas we were trying to sell, the ad men strange-looking in camouflage. I remember the hunt of the chase, the beauty of the animals, the fire of the shot, the chase of the sale. I never once fired my gun or managed to pitch anything on the trip; it was enough to get close to the beasts and to feel the power of sharing the earth with these animals, to know the smell of those green hills.

She counts her money and I don't wait for her to turn around. "See, the thing is, I feel like there are things we've just got to share, I just know it. It doesn't make any sense, it doesn't, but there's something here."

The room is almost empty now, the crowd thinned to the staff and a few drunkards trying to find the door, car keys being exchanged, coats pulled from their hooks. When the door opens, there is a sea of headlights, music blaring, laughter. I want to go home.

I move the barstool beside her and lean in to the bar near her.

"There's this place around the corner from here. It's dirty and it's cheap, but I know it's open. Let's share one cup of coffee."

She keeps counting her money and looking the other way, and I am the only person left in the bar. I put my coat on and take my keys out of my pocket.

"I'll go there and wait for you. I hope you'll come."

When I get back to the old truck, I lean against it for a long time. I watch as the cars pull out of the parking lot and everything circles around me—thoughts, images, a slight melancholy above and below me. I feel joy in my bones and slight suspicion, the world suddenly so new and foreign.

I wonder if she'll come or if she'll stay away, and I realize it doesn't matter all that much, the curves in the road. You just have to lean with them and do your best to see them coming. Still, I crave her, long for her, feel the euphoria when I think of the possibility. It is the kind of joy that stands alone.

I turn the engine on and travel the two blocks south to the diner on the corner, the Lenox Café, a square building hanging back from the road, bright and angular. I push the accelerator softly and pull into a parking spot, but I stay in the truck, rest my head on the steering wheel, fold my feet below me.

It is close to four in the morning, and I don't know how long I've been sitting there but I can feel the sky changing outside, the dark blue changing to a gray, the sun beginning to stretch its arms.

I hear a car pull up beside me, its lights dimmed, see her shadow inside. I feel adrenaline hit my veins, and I am alert and awake, I can feel the stubble on my face. I pull the keys from the ignition and step out to the sidewalk to meet her, rub my hands together for electricity.

"Hi, I'm Carmine." I speak loudly, as though I am still at the bar, stretching my words out so that she can read my lips. I shove my hands in my pockets and smile. I can see her eyes searching mine for something, but her mouth remains closed, her body stiff.

The clouds part above us, and I watch as she catches a chill and shivers from her spine.

"I'm Z, short for Zaire. It's cold out here; let's go in." She's wearing a red sweater that wraps around her body and the same jeans from the bar; she is taller in the light than in the dark.

The lights inside the diner are bright, and I squint as I follow her to a table in the corner with brown vinyl chairs and a red ketchup bottle in the center of the table.

For the first few minutes at the table, we both stare at the crack in the center of the Formica, reading its lines as though it is a palm telling our future, branching out in either direction, determining our fate. I pretend to look at the menu and study the pictures of eggs and salads and burgers and feel her from across the table, shifting in her seat, staring at the glossy menu, the pictures reflecting in the glass of her eyes.

"You know, I've never had coffee with a black woman before." As soon as the last word leaves my mouth, I can't believe I've said it. My hand moves to my face to try to somehow push it back in.

She grabs her bag and gets up to leave. She moves so fast.

"I should have known. This is some kind of game, isn't it? Some kind of stupid dare or something, isn't it?" She's angry and she walks through the maze of the restaurant quickly on her way to the Honda. I get up and follow her.

"Wait, please wait. I'm sorry. It was a stupid thing to say. It was, I know it was. Can we give this another try? Trust me enough for one cup of coffee?"

She pauses at the front of the restaurant with her hand on the entrance door and she waits. When she turns around, her eyes are more focused and she looks right through me, the hurt flushing her cheeks, her bag folded under her arm.

"Listen, I'm not an exhibit at a museum and I don't give lessons on black history, so if that's what you're here for . . ."

I stop her sentence and touch her on the pointy part of her elbow gently. We look at each other for a long time, customers milling around us, the music above soothing, the smell of grease hanging in the air. We both stop and breathe, and when I let go of her arm, she walks back to the table behind me.

After the waitress has taken our coffee order, I look at her and smile and realize that something is different about her; she holds something back.

"Let's try this again, Z. I'm Carmine. Southern gentleman from Eton with better manners than I've shown you so far. I'm glad that you agreed to meet me here. You compel me for reasons I don't understand." I don't recognize my voice, the humility, the neutrality; I'm so used to commanding women, moving them like pegs on a board.

She pulls her sweater wrap around her tighter but doesn't say anything. She looks at me intently, her eyebrows curved, her lips pursed, but the remnants of some old hurt doesn't come out.

When the coffee comes, she busies herself with the cream and sugar and doesn't look up at me.

"I once had this big life in Dallas. I was once rich. I was once powerful. But now I don't have anything." I begin in the middle of the story, work my way to the present, try to keep talking so I can keep her close and still.

She listens, her hand cupping the mug, her shoulders folding in, her gaze soft and tender. This new feeling, I know what it means to share, envelops me and I let it.

I paint the landscape of life in Dallas, the midnight meals with Ma, the sounds of Pa's pain, college, the bus ride, today's breakfast, the vacancy of my future, how I've been visiting this old preacher at my pa's old church and about how I'm trying to learn about things like forgiveness. I watch my hands as they soar in the air and tell my stories as though I am conducting a symphony of instruments, telling each one just what to play.

As I talk, she listens, and her body softens; I feel the energy between us change from yellow and red to purple and blue. She continues to refill her coffee and constantly adjusts the cream in it, the color changing from dark brown to a smooth toffee, the spoon clinking on the edges of the ceramic cup.

I start to tell her the story about the boy in the warehouse, but then stop: I don't want to scare her away, to tell her everything, to turn myself completely inside out. I pick up the menu to order.

"Carmine, this has been nice, it really has, but I have to go now. I'll see you around, okay?" She gets up to leave and tosses a few dollar bills on the table, pulled from her back pocket. I watch each of her movements. I don't say anything, watch her get up and leave, mouth the word good-bye, and sigh deeply. I ask the waitress for another cup of coffee and stay in the booth until the sun comes up.

Chapter 13

I WAKE UP THE next morning to Ma screaming my name over and over, first loudly, then it fades to a soft sound, each syllable of my name rushing out of her mouth loudly but dry. I come out of a deep sleep and feel it rushing through me.

I sit up in bed. Stop breathing. Wait. I am not sure if it is a dream I am still in or something else completely. Outside I can hear birds chirping from nests, and it all sounds the same, another morning regurgitated again, but not.

I hear footsteps coming down the hallway and then my door pushes open.

"Carmine, come fast, come fast. He's not gonna make it, he's not gonna make it." She's sobbing into her hands and pointing toward their room with one hand, the other holds her face, covers her mouth, part of her eye.

I pull my legs out of bed and push to the edge. I want to know how people push one foot in front of the other at times like this. The floor feels cold on my feet.

Ma still stands at my door. Time is in slow motion; it crawls from one moment to the next. I've never seen her face like this before. It's red-hot; her wrinkles are piled up under her eyes. I don't know what I'm supposed to do. I am the boy, she is the mother.

"Okay, Ma, okay. What's happened? Is Pa okay?"

She slides down to the floor and holds her face with both hands now, the sobs turning into moans. I feel like I'm caught in the wild, a herd of coyotes circling me; there's nowhere to go.

"He's . . . I think he's stopped breathing, Carmine, I think he's gone . . ." She stands up and looks at me, her eyes glassy and red; something has already left them. She's trying to compose herself.

"What do you mean, Ma? I just heard his bed squeak a little while ago."

"I went in there this morning to bring him his coffee like I always do, and he didn't move when I called his name, and Carmine, his skin is so cold, his skin is so cold. How long has it been? Where have we been? Where did he go?"

I pull on a pair of socks, then shoes; it seems like the thing I should do. Ma pulls her hands from her face and takes a deep breath, straightens her dress, watches my every move.

"I knew he was gonna go soon, Carmine, I knew he was gonna go soon, but . . ." She's crying again. I pull the long-sleeved shirt from the back of the chair and go to her.

"It's okay, Ma, it's okay." I hug her, look down the long hallway beyond her, tap the wood paneling in my room, and walk out.

The house is so quiet. It's barely after seven in the morning. I can feel the heat of the sun begin to warm the house, first the floors and then the walls; it's all a process. Without thinking, I remember Z's red sweater, the feel of it on my arm as I walked near her; does this thing now separate me from her, or is it all the same?

I can smell the coffee; the whole house is filled with it. I walk toward Pa's room and think about all the board meetings I've walked into, how many executives I've charmed, all the money I've made and the things I've owned—how none of it can help me at all right now.

My pajama bottoms drag on the floor, and I pause right in front of his door. I can see the dry, callused feet sticking out of the blanket; he lies flat on his back, his arms beside him. The blue comforter is the same one I remember; I don't know how these things don't just disintegrate with time, they just keep going.

I walk closer to the bed. I feel something moving, something aroused. Pa is alive. I pick up his wrist and feel the ashy skin in my hands. I find his pulse and count the distant beats.

I turn around and see Ma standing in the doorway. Her shoulders are stiff and her fingers are in her mouth; she waits for me to tell her something and I am surprised. Somehow I always thought it was them against me.

"Ma, he's still alive, he's not gone." I drop Pa's hand and walk away from the bed.

It had all been written out months before I got here. "Let me die, just let me die." I'd heard him say it at least a hundred times since, and Ma had it written up, a hand-scribbled note Pa'd tucked under his mattress. He wasn't one for lawyers.

I pass her on my way to the kitchen and think about what I want for breakfast. This day will be long, it will be arduous, it will change everything. I always thought the bend in the road would be seen miles before, a road sign, road curves sharply, then time would be going in a whole other direction.

I move some pans around and put bread in the toaster and crack an egg and fill up a coffee cup twice and do small circles in the kitchen, shuffling from the stove to the refrigerator to the table and back.

When I finally sit down, I chew on a piece of toast, take my time first nibbling at the crust, then take in the soft buttery center of the bread. I pretend that this is all that there is.

I hear Ma in the hallway breathing and crying, and it's easy to think that it's just the TV blaring in the other room, that these are not my parts and not my people and that I can switch off the sounds at any moment.

I pick up my coffee mug and take a sip, hold it in my mouth, try to hear something coming from Pa's room.

I take the last triangle of bread and soak up the egg yolk that has slipped from the center of the plate, and I slide them both in my mouth. There's nothing else to do.

I put the plate in the sink and rinse out my cup before going back to them.

*   *   *

When I was a boy, I'd wished for Pa's death a thousand times. When he was at the pulpit, when he was in his shed working, when I heard him arguing with Ma in their room, most of all when he stepped out onto the front porch and called my name.

"Carmine, son, get in here. Get yourself on in here." He said it sweetly. I could have been mistaken; I know there was more to him even then.

Sometimes he'd get up at the pulpit on Sunday mornings and he would seem to me like Jesus himself, wise, the son of God all along and nobody knew it. Then we'd get home after service and he'd pick up a drink or backhand me for something or just turn his face when I looked to him, point at the Book, there were so many ways that he ran from me.

In my room, I'd plot. Sometimes I thought about messing with the brake lines in his old truck; other times I'd thought of asking kids at school to jump him; on really angry days, I would think of taking a kitchen knife to him myself, stabbing him in the gut; but sometimes I'd just wish he and Ma would move away, never telling me where they'd gone and if they'd ever come back. This one was my favorite fantasy. I'd often wake up and first thing pull the shades back on my bedroom window and look for that old truck. It was always there, but I never stopped sort of hoping.

Death makes you think about things in a different way. I mean, what life is and isn't. Death sorta brings all of this together, in one solitary place, you in a room with all of these things that belong to you.

I bring Ma a cup of coffee and sit on the floor with her in the hallway.

"One of us should be with him, Ma, one of us should be in there with him."

She stares off into space, and I pass my hand in front of her eyes.

"I don't want to say good-bye, Carmine. That's all he's waiting for—you and me to say our peace and tell him it's all right. If I stay out here, he won't go. I know he won't." She picks up the plastic mug and starts to take a sip, but can't. I see her eyes fill up with tears, and I take the cup from her.

"It's time, Ma, it's just time." I look toward the window at the end of the hallway and see the tree limbs move outside of it; the green leaves scrape the window and then brush across the roof. Everything has slowed down, a reel from an old home movie; we sit and we wait for the pacing to change and the story line to move along without us, but it never does.

"I'll go in first, Ma, I'll go in and talk to him and say what I want to say and tell him good-bye. I want to, Ma, I want to." I pull myself up and lean against the wall. I look down at the top of her gray head and wait for her to talk, but she never says anything.

I pull up the chair from the corner of the room, a small rickety piece Pa made many years ago, the first of a set that never came to be.

I push the chair up to the bed the same way I did a few weeks earlier. His mouth is slightly open and his lips are so dry and cracked that they look like they could start bleeding if he tried to talk. The oxygen rests just under his knees; it hums from the other side of the room.

I can hear Ma weeping in the doorway but I don't look back.

"I never asked what it was like for you, how things were when you were a boy, or if you actually believed all those things you'd say on Sunday mornings or late at night after you'd been drinking. I just assumed if you said them you meant them, and I learned to define life by those words."

I keep talking but my voice is barely above a whisper. I can see the tips of his shiny toes peeking out from the blanket, smell his sourness, feel the air hovering above us. Pa skips a breath and chokes a little; I can hear the phlegm move around in his chest; the machine hums without hesitation. I start to leave the room but I don't, grab the edge of the blanket to hold me, twist it. I want to ride this out. I have to.

I kneel down beside his bed and pause, put my face in my hands, and start talking.

"See, Pa, the thing is, I don't know what to do right now. I keep seeing this old preacher; he's the one at the church you used to lead. Have you seen him around? Well, he keeps telling me I've got to learn to forgive, forgive it all. But now you're dying.

"I've lived my life by taking and by hurting and by never apologizing or looking back or caring about any but my own self. And I've seen some stuff, some bad stuff.

"The preacher told me that all you have to do is take your sins to the Father. And I know he wasn't talking about you, but see, you've been the only father I've ever known, and if there truly is a Father up above, I haven't known him except through you, and I can't seem to make sense of my whole life and why it's been so hard to get love from either of you."

I pause for a long time, choke back tears, try to keep silent, wipe the sweat off my brow with my shirtsleeve.

"So what am I supposed to do now?" I walk to the end of the bed and rest my hands on the footboard, pull the blanket over Pa's feet, go back around to the side of the bed, and sit back in the chair.

I hear Ma moving around in the kitchen; the tips of her shoes hit the kitchen cabinet doors, and water runs.

I stare at his face. It's sullen; there is no color left in his skin. His eyes are closed, but I can see a sliver of his old self where his lids don't quite close, a white line and then the edges of his blue irises.

"I know you're still there. I know you can hear me. I know you *want* to hear me." I take off the sweatshirt I'm wearing and stare at his face again. Somehow expect he'll speak. His open mouth makes a small whistling sound as it pushes out the dry machine air, but that's it.

"I want you to know that I'm letting it all go, I mean it. I'm letting it all go. I will look at the past, but I won't stare at it anymore, Pa. I won't, and you don't either. You go, you go in peace, and I will, too. I will try to."

I reach out my hand and my fingers climb the bedsheets over to his arm and down to his hand. When I close my palm over his knuckles, I expect flames, I expect electricity, I expect my insides to fold in and die. Nothing happens. I squeeze his hand a little and then let go, cup my own face in my hands.

It had all happened so much easier than I thought it would, the end, I mean. I expected some kind of eponymous climax, a triumphant chorus of music, to somehow feel like a new person, or at least better about the old.

It was quiet, the air didn't change, the trees outside didn't stop to wait or hear and even the mailman slid the mail through the mail slot the same as always.

When I said my peace, finally said the thing I'd waited my whole life to say, I walk out of the room, I find Ma on the sofa, her face swollen and red, her body a stark desert.

She puts her arms around me and holds me. My hands are in my pockets and I wait, smell the top of her head, then put my arms around her.

She drops her arms to her side and walks to their room. I head to the kitchen and start washing the breakfast dishes.

CHAPTER 14

DAYS LATER, ON THE stairs of First Baptist Church of Eton, I am helping an elderly woman up the stairs. The small body is familiar but I can't quite place it: the lines in her face or her glassy blue eyes or the lean of her back. But I feel as though I should know. I'm losing my edge, its teeth blunt and no longer able to cut, my salesman charm fading like a picture left out in the rain. I think I've known her as a boy, but I can't be sure; I can't remember where I might have put her in my memory.

She leans on me for support and we walk up the old concrete steps of the church. I am wearing old jeans, my old leather jacket. I can feel the wind blow up my cuffs, in my spine; my cheeks are warm and my breath is hot. I worry my bones will fail me, but somehow I know they won't. Every muscle feels lengthened and strained and afraid of the grief, as though it's the enemy, bound to attack me at any moment. I don't yet know what it means to feel some of these things or if I need to feel them to really let any of them go.

"I'm sorry for your loss, son." She looks me in the face, and in her eyes I can see myself, ten years old and skinny, afraid to make eye contact with a group of women. I can now remember her bringing food and Christmas presents to us the year we'd moved back to Eton from Port Arthur and had nothing. I remember the potato casseroles and breads and fruitcake and gifts that had said "boy" and "small adult woman" and even for Pa, a flannel shirt in a box marked "large adult male."

When I get to the top of the stairs, I say my good-bye to her, tell her I remember how she took care of my family, that it's appreciated, then I walk in. Services will begin soon. Outside, dusk is leaning in, and I search my mind for all of the details Ma and I have discussed: grounds, flowers, thirty-two people to call. I search the halls of the church for the pastor and reach in my back pocket for my wallet.

At the church, I can't stand to sit in the pews and wait with Ma; for two days I have been by her side. When a couple of Pa's old friends stop to give their condolences, I head back to the front of the church to get some air.

Before I get to the door, I can see her at the bottom of the stairs; she's a stranger, but so familiar too. For days, she's been turning soft circles in my mind, without beginning or end, only up and down, the red sweater floating in the air, the clink of her spoon, the distance between us. She never did call.

I walk outside and wait for her to finish speaking to someone; her skin is the color of cocoa in the afternoon light. The sun is sliding beneath the hills in the east, the mosquitoes are looming, cars park in the distance, my stomach rumbles. I try so hard not to fall to the pavement.

"Excuse me." I look into her eyes for a long time before speaking. I don't want to say the wrong thing again; I don't want to break.

"Hey . . . I mean hi." I hold onto the railing.

"What are you doing here? Aren't you going back to Dallas?" She smiles.

"Eton's home for me now. Eton, Georgia, population 318, well, 319 now. Well, with my pa gone and me back, I guess it evens things out now, doesn't it? What are you doing here?"

"I have family here in Eton. I actually spent most of my childhood summers here. I know these back roads well. Sometimes I drive in and go to church with my aunt on Sunday nights. I wasn't expecting to see you here . . ."

"Really? You spent summers here? How is it possible that we never ran into each other?" In that moment, I remember

Eric, how I so easily walked away. The shame pulls me down by the neck.

"Luck, I guess."

"I am about to bury my pa." I push a rock off the edge of the stairs and look up.

"I'm so sorry to hear that. I remember you telling me how sick he's been. What will you do here now?" She fidgets, pulls her bag back onto her shoulder, shifts her weight to one hip.

"Well, it's all still coming together, but I think I'm going to take over my father's furniture-making business. Help my ma out; take it slow for a while."

We stand there for a minute or so, looking at each other, watching people as they pass by, up the stairs and into the church.

"Good luck to you." She lets her eyes linger for a few moments before grabbing the rail of the stairs and heading into the church.

"Would you like to get together sometime? I could use a friend right now. Do people actually say that? Let's go fly a kite? Row down the river? Eat pecan pie? Ice cream—it doesn't matter what we do. Can we be friends?"

"I don't know . . ." She softens her tone and leans into me a little.

I take a couple steps closer to her. "You've got nothing to lose but a little more time. Plus, I've spilled my guts to you so you know what I'm about. What's there to fear? Can we meet after services tonight?"

"How about first thing in the morning. I'm not driving back to Atlanta until tomorrow night."

"Okay. What time? Where?"

"Let's meet on these steps again at noon."

"Okay." I turn to walk up the stairs and look back at her one last time.

She smiles.

"Carmine, I will be thinking of you and your family."

*   *   *

Pa's service begins at nightfall, just the way he wanted it. I can hear the crickets outside the clapboard walls, humming and singing; they do what they do the same every night, their bodies tapping the windows, they want out or in, they don't know which, they don't know any better than we do. Eton moves slowly beyond the sounds of the church's organ, and people complain and work in their lawns and push food around on plates. I don't know what to do with how this feels. I don't know if I'm supposed to run from it or let it climb on me.

When the pastor begins to speak, I cannot take my eyes off his mouth: his syllables leave his chest and come out in long sounds, stretching in front of him and echoing, and he tells all sixteen of us how dust turns to dust and endings are beginnings. On and on it seems to go. Ma sits next to me sniffling, looking off into the distance, somewhere beyond the pulpit.

I don't plan to get up to speak, but when there's a pause in the sermon and Ma looks over to me, I stand and raise my hand. I can't let this end, let him leave so easily.

"I do have a few words," I say, as though I am talking to myself, the words pushing at the backs of my legs until I stand on the pulpit in my shirt and tie.

The church is so quiet, and the few faces within it so empty, an old neighbor, a past parishioner, the man from the lumberyard where Pa always bought his wood, then Pa's drinking buddy, Ralph. No one sits on the same pew, and they are scattered like squares of an old quilt, nothing alike but in the same place and the same time and for the same reason. Stanley takes a seat in the front row and looks at me.

I pause for a long time and try not to put my face in my hands, let the tears run down my face and squint. Is this who I've always been beneath it all? I squeeze the side of the podium and wait for Ma to look up; I am still someone's son, that has always been true.

A week ago we sat in the living room and ate grapes and old meatloaf and cold mashed potatoes and orange jellied candies, and I remember looking up and seeing Pa leaning on his cane in the doorway of his room watching us. His face sagging and somber, a slight glow around him, I saw him for the first time since I'd arrived. The sight of him made me hold my breath for a few seconds, made me fall into the back of the sofa.

My hands shake as I stand at the pulpit and look at Stanley, try to pull together a few calm words. I am crying now and I can't stop; a flood of memories slide past my eyes and then leave, it's all coming so fast.

I look around and remember when Pa'd been removed from this very same church for being drunk one too many Sunday mornings and that he left without a word. I don't think he ever believed in God after that, as though his faith was attached to some guarantee, the two of them parting ways, Pa giving up for good. I left shortly after that and never remember him being anything other than the angry man walking out the church doors or yelling late into the night or holing up in that shed in a cloud of sawdust.

But now I see him in that light, that warm and hazy light, a man, a body, both broken. I can barely remember the man I was in Dallas. How is it possible to be one thing, then another? What will I turn out to be after all?

"I want to say something good about my old man; I want to tell you stories; I want to say that life won't be the same without him—but I can't. I don't even know how much I really loved him. But I forgive him for the trouble he made. I won't spend another second hating him, and that's got to be a little like love."

I look out over the pews and stop crying for a moment; a kind of soft peace slides over me and my shoulders fall. I find Pastor Stanley's eyes, then Ma's. I can see a sliver of the moon outside one of the tall windows.

After the service, old friends come up to me. Tell me stories about Pa, how he used to dance the jig, how he used to wear his pants too short, how his hair was the color of cotton when he was little, how he once gave a man CPR and saved him from death.

The neighbor, Lucy, the one that lives on the corner, comes up to me last and takes my hand in hers. Her hair is the same color as the other Lucy, the one on TV, and she smiles, her pale, wrinkly skin coming close to me. Her perfume reminds me of the cosmetic counter at Dillard's.

"I enjoyed your eulogy, son, I did. People don't realize that a man is just a man and nothing more, and he can't always help that now, can he?" She goes on to tell me how she watched me grow up and how lost my parents were after I left home, how Pa used to mow her grass on Saturday mornings. I stare at her while she speaks and listen to each word as it comes out of her mouth, the pieces falling together into a picture.

*   *   *

An hour later, Ma and I drive home. The mortuary has come to collect Pa's body for cremation. It all ended so neatly.

Eton is quiet and serene, almost no one on the narrow roads as we drive through town. The windows are down, and I breathe in the mountain air, cold in my chest; the space between my mother and me feels delicate now.

I park the old truck in the drive and walk around to help her out; she leans in to me, more brittle than the day before, and she sighs so deeply that my legs bend at the knees from her weight and I have to grab the side of the truck for support.

"Come on, Ma." I put my arm around her shoulders. When I unlock the front door, the yellow light of the lamp greets us and we sit down on the sofa together. The house is so quiet, nothing but the buzz of the refrigerator coming from the kitchen, a few bugs hitting the glass of the windows. I want a drink, but let it go. I look at Ma's face for a long time.

"Don't worry, Ma, I'll stay around. You won't be alone."

I see a tear roll down her pale face, but she doesn't say anything. Her foot taps the floor and she grabs the TV remote.

"Get me a blanket out of the hall closet, would you?" She lays her head on the end of the couch. I get the blanket and cover her.

CHAPTER 15

I CAN'T SLEEP THAT night; think about Pa, Z, everyone I've ever known, see all of this space in front of me with no clear path. I wonder when it'll be shown.

When I step out of my room to leave in the morning, Ma is on her corner of the sofa. When she looks up at me, a little more of her gone, her eyes look gray and absent.

"Did you eat, Ma?"

She takes a sip of coffee and holds her breath a minute before replying.

"I had a piece of toast with jam. Didn't sleep a wink. It's like my mind was searching this house for him, you know what I mean?" She crosses one leg over the other and smiles at me weakly, turns away.

"I know, Ma. It's gonna take some time, maybe a lot of time, to get used to the idea." I take her coffee cup from her hand and take it to the kitchen to refill it.

"I'm heading out for a while, okay?" I tell her as I hand her cup back to her. "But I'll be back soon."

She smiles and waves her hand at me as she lights up a cigarette.

*   *   *

I am walking up to the steps of the church when I see her there. The sun is high and bright, and I have to squint hard to see her completely, but there she is, sitting on the stairs, her legs folded beneath her, in a white strappy shirt with the same red sweater on her shoulders.

"Good morning," I say, and I sit down beside her and look into her eyes for a long time. She smiles slightly, understands me, I think, and then looks away. The building is silent behind us, and we sit still for a long time. It's the longest I've ever sat still, I think, in the presence of another human, and it is slightly uncomfortable.

"This is for you." I hand her a long-stemmed sunflower.

She takes me in, one piece at a time, and says thank you.

She runs her hands up and down her jeans. I can hear the soft sound of the material, her long brown fingers kneading the muscles in her thighs; I smell honeysuckle nearby.

She stands up and looks down at me.

"So, what do you want to do today?" She is so tall, a steeple, a woman; my insides relax, fold, but my palms begin to sweat. I stand up and look her in the eyes.

"Let's go to the park," she says, pushing her bag over her shoulder. When she starts walking toward a white Honda, I follow.

"Get in. I'll drive us." She's behind the wheel as I climb into the car beside her, see my shadow cast across the dash. I feel like I float above my body, the real me watching this new version of myself trying to figure out what he's doing.

She puts the windows down and the car in drive, and I smell the honeysuckle again, the leather of my jacket, count the bumps of her knuckles on the steering wheel.

"I'm just curious . . . why did you decide to come out with me anyway? You left so abruptly the other night."

She's looking straight ahead at the road, and I can see her smile as she seems to count the cars on the road. She takes a deep breath before answering me.

"Carmine, the truth is, I really don't know. I just . . . I just thought I'd take a chance on this." She taps the wheel and smiles again and fidgets in her seat. I remember a girl in first grade that I loved, soft and sweet and amiable like this.

I tell her, "I don't really understand anything right now, only that maybe that's okay for once. I'm trying to figure out how I can start over, if it's even possible, or if you have to keep what you have to make it something new. I am not making any sense, am I?"

"No, I get it, I do, I know what you mean." She pulls into a parking space near a green slope of hill at the park and then looks at me. Her eyes seem afraid but wide-open.

We get out and she pulls a picnic basket out of the trunk of her car. The wicker is old and swollen, and inside she has tucked a few things: wine and a tray of cheeses and a wedge of French bread. At the bottom of the basket is a book of poetry by Rumi.

"I put a few things together for us," she tells me as she walks toward the hill.

In the distance, we can hear children playing, their joy echoing through the fall air. There are trees all around us, and on a field to the left, a group of men play soccer.

We sit down on the green grass and fold our legs beneath us. She takes a few things from the basket and hands me a glass of wine, puts some crackers and cheese on a paper plate, rests on her back and elbows in the grass. The sky is a tender blue above us.

I pick up the book of poetry and flip through the pages. The wind blows between us, soft. I can feel our differences, our pasts circling around us.

"'Out beyond ideas of wrongdoing and rightdoing, there is a field. I'll meet you there.'" I run my pale finger over the black font of the letters . . . pause on some of the words . . . out . . . wrongdoing . . . you and there. I don't ever remember reading a poem in my life.

"Do you think there is such a space?" I ask her.

She pops a grape in her mouth and starts to talk.

"I'd like to think there is, but I don't know."

A small girl runs past us with a kite; it's purple and pink colors trailing after her. We both smile.

I move closer to her and smell her skin, laundry detergent, the faint smell of plastic strawberry on her lips. I reach out and touch her hand, feel her tense, then relax, myself tremble. I want to be close to her so bad.

I start thinking about Dallas and remember the power, the glory, and I worry that the old Carmine is trying to slip back. It would be easier to be that than this.

"So, what do you do in Atlanta, Z? I mean, besides working at the club." I adjust my feet, cross my legs in the grass, breathe deeply, and listen closely for my old words, watch carefully so they don't slip from my mouth.

She rubs her hand over her jeans again. Squints in the sunlight. Her mouth is rich.

"I love Atlanta, exploring it, checking out little shops. I love the way the city vibrates and moves so fast. I like that energy. I sing, too, but not the way you heard me in the club that night." She takes a sip of wine and looks around, stretches out, and continues talking.

"When I was a girl, my daddy used to ask me to sing, and it made me feel so special, so important. I drive to Eton sometimes just so my Aunt Tina can tell me stories about my father, her younger brother, and sometimes when we sit in her old foyer, I'm hoping that she'll ask me to sing the way that he did so I can remember what it was like." She gets lost for a minute, smiles as she remembers, then straightens up as she remembers the present.

We relax, and for the next couple of hours, we talk about our fathers, and she tells me how hers was mostly absent but so loving and I tell her about Pa's anger, and as we do, the wind picks up and blows at us. Sometimes as she's speaking, her hands make big circles in the air and she forgets that she can't trust me, and I tell her about how the numbness has been wearing off, how my whole life was an escape plan, and I feel like what a waste. I tell her how Pa's death has affected me, how it has made me question the things I held onto for so many years, the things I coveted, the things I hid from. "What is the truth?" I ask her.

"I think a family is a circle, a ring, and when there's a death, the circle has to change, things 'have' to shift. For me, when my father left us, I suddenly felt as though I didn't know who I was anymore, as if I existed in his eyes only, how he saw me. I'm still trying to figure it out, who I really am, if I'm at all like he thought I was. I still want to know why it was so easy for him to pop in and out of our lives as though it didn't matter."

We go back and forth like that. Why did he do this, you think, and how could she do that?

As the sun starts to set over the trees, we begin to fade and realize how much we have in common, how much we've shared. Sometimes the thought gives me a sense of panic, where is the control? Other times, I can see myself sinking into it, swimming in it.

When the streetlights pop on, we get up and start to pack everything up. I escape back into my mind, but notice her every move, how her shoulders curve in and her toes are painted red.

"When will you drive back to Atlanta?" I ask her as we walk back to the car. She seems far away again, with the sun gone, the contents of her mind different now.

"I think I'll drive back to Atlanta tonight just to be in my own space." She taps the steering wheel and then starts the engine. I zip up my coat, watch people packing up, kids heading home through the hills, taking shortcuts through the woods. She backs the car out of the parking lot and turns the radio on.

"Can I call you?" I ask, reach my hand out to touch her arm. The air in the car is warm. She doesn't pull away this time.

"How about I call you?" The shapes of her eyes are more oval now as they look directly at me. She smiles and then looks back at the road.

I agree, say sure, keep quiet for the rest of the way home.

"Bye, Carmine," she says as she pulls in front of the church to let me out.

I stand by the stairs for a very long time and look up at the Eton sky, full of clouds and stars and mystery.

*   *   *

For the next few days, Ma and I don't know what to do with ourselves. We walk from room to room, wandering listlessly, sometimes passing each other by with a short glance. Sometimes Ma makes heavy comments that I don't know what to do with.

"Carmine, son, it feels as though I've lost not one limb, but two, an arm and a leg. What am I supposed to do, son?"

Her pale dresses hang off her bony shoulders even more lately. I want her to live.

Sometimes I feel moments of terror, as though the floor will disappear beneath me. Other times a feeling of euphoria comes over me, and I want to jump and laugh and punch circles in the air because I am finally rid of him. Then a certain melancholy comes over me, as though nothing really holds me to the ground anymore.

I pull out my old resumes and consider my options again. Dallas has become but a phantom in my mind, but I know it still exists. The lights, the action, it wouldn't take much to slip back into the man I was.

There is the East Coast, there are Europe and South America and anyplace on the globe, really. My career, my reputation precedes me, but then what? I don't know if I can stand for those things anymore, I've seen the puppet strings; but I don't know if I can be the man that cares for his old mother, chops wood, and counts the blinking stoplights.

Chapter 16

I DRIVE INTO ATLANTA in that old truck. The day is overshadowed by clouds and voices in the city, and it reminds me of Dallas, the energy flowing in and out of tunnels within the city, the people, the ants foraging and gathering; it's all the same wherever you go, that kind of energy, the color purple, the heat of red, all that getting. On the seat beside me I've brought a few things for us: a bag of oranges, a bottle of Martin Ray wine, a box of old wooden dominoes I found in Pa's shed. I'm wearing a blue shirt with the sleeves rolled up, and I'm so aware of everything around me, the possibility of the future, the old boundaries of myself smudged out by a big old eraser, grief maybe, or age; maybe the grit is finally something good. I park the old truck in front of her building.

She lives in an eclectic part of the city on a hill with color everywhere, but the buildings are plain and the trees short and the noise here somehow different, a mumble beneath it all, a whisper, a rustle under the covers, then the sound of a car. A block away I see some children playing with water guns, and to the right there is an old woman in front of her apartment clipping plants, and below a puddle drains into the nearby gutter. I step out of the truck and look up. Z is leaning out of the window on the third floor watching me. She smiles wide, and I can see all of her teeth and feel the breadth of her, open here, and free. I am surprised and intimidated and ready to try again. She points to the big main door of her building. I walk in. I put the sack of oranges under my arm and the wine and dominoes in the other.

She opens the door to greet me, and I tell her that I'm glad she called. She moves things around in the kitchen and around the apartment. I watch her move in the light of her space, so different from the club, and when I stop talking, she forgets I'm there for a few moments and begins to hum.

An hour later we are sitting on the living room floor with boxes lined up around us. She's just moved in. We eat homemade tortellini and drink the wine. Outside, the kids still play, cars pass, time becomes easier.

"Listen, it means a lot that you invited me here tonight. It feels so good to have some company other than Ma's. Things have been tough lately; I'm just doing my best to take it day by day, you know?"

"Yes, it's special when two people can meet each other in the present somehow, some way, and let that be enough. I mean, when they can share what's real." She looks away and then back, squints her eyes at me, and fills up her water glass. She wants to believe, I can feel it. Outside I think I can hear the ants foraging and searching up and down her block. I feel like one of them. I want to carry something home.

I see a box of photos, some with Z's face in them, some with old men on fishing boats, others black-and-white square images with a family's history to them.

"Now that's what I call a fish." I smile. Remembering our family photos at home, I'm surprised at the symmetry here.

"Yeah, Little River, my family; there's lots to share. We were sent to live with my grandparents in Little River, South Carolina. Granddaddy was a fisherman. Little River is an old fishing village—the best seafood, the greatest blue crab festival, and live oak trees that are at least a hundred years old. It's a peaceful slow-paced town filled with fishermen and shrimpers and a quieter, simpler way of life, not that much different than Eton, I guess."

She sighs, rubs the back of her neck. Outside, the sun goes down and the streetlights come on. Her windows are open, and a breeze fills the room.

"It looks special. I'd love to visit one day—go shark fishing."

"Shark fishing . . . I'm not sure that's the place." She laughs, tilts her head to one side.

"Just so you know, Little River has both onshore as well as deep fishing in the Gulf Stream. Surprised?" I sit up straighter and look at her.

"You? I thought you were all looks and charm. You got smarts, too?" She smiles broadly, relaxes a little.

"There's a little more to me than that—I think, anyway. Are you close to your family?" I ask her. I think for a second about what family means to me.

"I guess you can say that. Do you have any siblings?" She sits Indian style, rubs her hands over her ankles.

"Nope. I'm an only child. What about you?"

"Ha." She pauses, counting the tips of her fingers. "Well, that's a complicated question. There are twelve of us . . . so far."

"You're kidding, right?" I laugh.

"Well, there are four of us, three sisters and my brother, and then a bunch of brothers and sisters from my dad's side. I grew up with just four of us though."

I smile at her seductively. "What was your family like? Your parents?"

"We used to be . . . we had nothing growing up, and my mom never worked but she somehow always fed us. What about you? I bet it was fun growing up in a small town."

"Something happened when we left Port Arthur."

"Port Arthur?"

"Texas. Nothing ever seemed to work, you know?"

"Why'd you leave Port Arthur?"

"My grandfather owned an old boat in Port Arthur—it's a seaport; he made money from his fishing boat for years. Worked the waters and weathered with the boat and lived a life he loved, you know. When he passed, my pa somehow managed to gamble everything away. You wouldn't believe it, but he did it so fast, without thinking, without remembering, like none of it even mattered . . . . After that, he wanted to leave all that behind to start afresh, here in Eton. The rest is history pretty much."

"So why Dallas? I mean, how did you get from here to there?"

"I wanted to leave Eton from as far back as I can remember—Eton is country, just country, nothing like Dallas. There is nowhere to hide."

"What's the difference?" She looks at me coyly.

I grab her by the shoulders, shake her, smile; it feels good to talk about something lighter. "Blasphemous!"

"Dallas is where folks go to hide from the rest of the world, huh?" She takes a drink of wine and gets up and changes the music, something by Nina Simone.

"It is a good place to hide, but really you can hide anywhere, if that's what you want to do." I say it with confidence, like I've always known it.

"So, when are you leaving purgatory for paradise?"

"Not for quite a while, I imagine. Call it a hunch. This place has got a hold on me."

"But Eton? Not Atlanta? Not California? Can you really imagine yourself settling in Eton?"

"I don't know; I just have a feeling that this is where I need to be, at least for now. I don't know about forever. Do we ever really know anyway?"

"There's comfort in keeping things simple. I know that much is true." She smiles at me so softly, and I get a glimpse of how her face must have looked as a girl.

"Yes, I'm learning that, but I miss Dallas big-time. Daddy Jack's Wood Grill—the best Jim Beam steak, I oughta make you some. Austin Hill country, good ol' Texas blues, songs of obscure wisdom, the rodeo, Texas rain showers, jubilee, and the best damn dancing in the whole world."

"Jubilee? You mean a hoedown? I don't think so."

"Don't knock it till you've tried it. I think you'd like it. You've got it all in your bones: Janis, Billie, Aretha. They've all done the jubilee."

"I'd be lynched." She laughs.

"It's just a big country concert. Seriously!"

I reach in to kiss her. She pulls away.

"How come the conversation always come back to me? I am an open book. I turned every page for you, but you don't give me much."

I reach out and put my hand on her arm. Want to touch her face. Wait for her to talk.

"You're not the only broken one, Carmine. I've got history, it's no secret. I want to meet you in this space, but it's hard to trust you." She gets up and takes the dishes to the kitchen. She comes back, lights a red candle, and starts talking again. "I've always loved men. I knew their presence meant Mom would leave me alone, it meant money, it meant Dad coming home, it always means something good or bad . . . and I kinda feel the same about you."

We hear a loud siren on the street below, listen as it passes in front of the building and then turns a few streets down and fades away.

"We had nothing growing up . . . my mom hustled to feed us. She made us hustle too. Everything came day by day. I stayed in school in spite of it all, did my best, then moved to Atlanta to go to college. I couldn't get either one of my parents to show up and sign anything, not even to get me free money for school, so I tried to pay for it myself. I started school, took a job, began to hustle where I could. I made an agreement with myself always to have money to pay for everything, and I've been on my own for years now."

"I love these things about you," I tell her. She's in a new zone, so free; the candle flickers on and off her face, and her eyes look off somewhere in the distance.

"It's funny how time flies . . . I wanted to learn to play the piano, speak and sing in French like Billie or Josephine, the old blues singers . . . so many ways to be me."

"I just remember always being hungry as a child. We'd go to the grocery store, and my mom would open up a loaf of bread and hand the slices out to us, no kidding. She'd open up turkey, cheese—American Kraft singles—and we'd make our sandwiches and drink soda right there in the store and then leave." She laughs nervously, walks to the kitchen and washes her hands, sits back down.

"My mother was always on something—Topamax, Ativan—she was fun at times, but often she'd get upset, yell and scream at the slightest mistake. We could never really relax, you know?

"Sometimes she'd break down and cry, wishing she had done things differently, call us mistakes. In those moments I felt a feeling that I wasn't used to; she was the child and I the mother trying to calm her, trying to let her know everything was going to be okay. I wanted it to be so different; I wanted so much more."

I lean in to her, reach for her hand, rest my palm on her knee instead. A plane passes overhead, and we both look up and listen to it for a few moments. It is after midnight now, but a new energy is in her.

"I didn't really know my dad . . . he'd come by the house every six months or so, seems like he came around a handful of times my whole life, cause a lot of trouble and leave. I don't know if he loved us; I know he sometimes felt responsible for us, but not enough to stay."

She is breathless, but keeps going, tells me about Little River, spending summers with her grandparents, the light and airy days with nothing to do, the fragrant memories of Granmama's old trunk, eating as much chocolate as any one child could, the sound of the piano's melody throughout the house. Then she stops. Takes a deep breath in and gets up from the floor.

She goes into the bedroom and starts unpacking boxes, the music of Nina Simone plays; I don't know what I'm supposed to do.

I walk up behind her, lean my head on her shoulders, watch her hands go in and out of the cardboard box, feel the chill of the room.

She pushes the box away and stands still. The music clicks off, and the only thing we hear are summer bugs slapping against the window.

"You know, I haven't always been what I could be, but I'm trying, want to see what I really am. It's begun with you," I tell her. "Don't you want to know what's possible, too? To see if life can be good?"

She pulls away from me and goes back to the living room. She pulls a big floor pillow from the corner of the room and sits on it. I sit down beside her, grab her hand; the pillow feels like velvet, a magic carpet. I pull her close to me, and she lets me.

I sigh into her hair, nod my head, take in her musk, and feel her heart beating fast.

"I can give you one day at a time, one day at a time. Okay?" She leans into me.

Chapter 17

A FEW DAYS LATER, I show up at her door again. I am laughing when she answers the door wearing a soft sundress. I suck in my breath.

"Hi. What are you doing here?" she asks quietly, leaning her weight on one hip. I can hear the sound of her building reverberating, a crying baby a few floors up, a vacuum cleaner somewhere below us, the smell of a beefy stew in the air.

"This is for you," I say, handing her a flier I found tacked to a telephone pole yesterday morning. "Your official invitation to the best hoedown east of the Mississippi."

Before she can answer, I hand her a box, a white cardboard thing with a pink bow wrapped around it. She takes it and smiles.

"Carmine . . ." She opens the box. It's a wicker cowboy hat.

She chuckles out loud, and I smile broadly. I got her, I think; I managed to shock her in the right way.

"This is so . . ." She doesn't complete her thought.

"Corny. Yes, I know, but why don't you put it on and go heehawing with me?"

A half hour later, we walk out to the street. The sundress she's wearing flows playfully to the middle of her thighs. I'm glad she didn't change. The print is innocuous enough: round sunflowers, inches from one another, covering the palest of white material. The straps barely hold up the fullness of her breasts, and I try not to stare. Under the hat, her face is flawless in just lip gloss and mascara.

There are people on the street. A young mother with a toddler walking slowly beside her, an elderly man with a small dog; we watch them as they watch us.

It is a warm day, with soft winds and smells, and she keeps her window down in the truck as we drive back to the country.

"What are you thinking about?" I ask her, merging onto the highway back toward Eton. I fiddle with the radio, searching for neutrality, suddenly feel off-center.

"Oh nothing," she says. "I'm just wondering why you have such a big truck." She laughs and turns up the radio.

*   *   *

The Chatsworth jubilee is big and full, even by Dallas standards, and the crowd rests on top of a hillside not far from Eton; there is a scent of lavender in the air. There are people everywhere, upon the hills, laying in the grass, babies and seniors, families and singles; it's a melting pot.

I've managed to pull it together for us this time. I have a blanket, a cooler full of beers, a handful of wildflowers for her. I sigh as I pull it all out of the bed of the truck.

"I'm impressed. Your mama did teach you something, I see." Her eyebrows raise with her words.

"Yeah, I manage okay, some of the time," I say as I find us an open spot under a small tree. In the distance, the band has started, sounds like Juice Newton performing "Ride'Em Cowboy."

The night unfolds much like the song, literally, piece by piece, lyrical at times, sometimes fast and sometimes too slow. We hear the nuances of the fiddle as the clouds begin to cover the sky, the smell of barbeque, kids out of breath and laughing; there is no place but here.

At some point I pull her up off the blanket, wrap my arms around her, and show her how it's done. I don't remember ever being this playful.

"Let me show you the two-step, darlin'," I say as I swing her around. Her head falls back in laughter, and I can't believe how easily she's letting me push her around the grass, pushing her feet in the right direction with my knees.

A few hours go by and we dance, laugh. I teach her the words to the craggiest of country songs, and she pretends not to like it, says they're all depressing, all about lost wives and horses, sound like broken washing machines, she says. I don't think about Ma even once, or Pa's raspy breathing, not even the Dallas skyline or the money I could be making right now, or what the next day might hold.

After the last song of the night, we fall breathlessly onto the ground, and I reach over and cover her with the side of the blanket, move in closer to her, hand her a cold beer. The sun has fallen behind the hills, and the air has a chill to it now.

I love the way her skin smells, so ripe and sweet, so soft; I try to hold myself back. My face is just a few inches from hers; our eyes meet for a second, I turn away. The magnetism is strong. Playfully, she pushes my hat over my face. I take it off and push hers off, lean forward and whisper into her ear, "I've been here with you a million times."

"You're all right by me," she tells me, meeting my eyes again for a second longer this time before looking up at the sky, playfully pushing me away.

We stay for a while longer, watch as the crowds thin and people leave the hills and head home.

"Let's get out of here," I say as I lean closer and brush her lips with mine.

She nods.

On the ride home, we don't talk much, my eyes focus on the lines of the road, one dashed line at a time. She rolls down her window and lets her fingers flutter in the wind like she's playing music.

When I park the truck in front of her building, I follow her up the stairs to her apartment, hover near her as she fumbles with the lock on her front door, feel her begin to shake as I slide the straps of her dress over her shoulders.

As soon as the door pushes open, I take her face in my hands and just breathe with her for a few moments. The apartment is cold and dusty and dark. I'd imagined just how this might unfold, making love instead of screwing, intimacy instead of flight, but animal instincts must be forgiven and I push forward.

My hands reach under her dress and slide up and down her; she seems to melt, finds my lips and presses her mouth so hard I can barely breathe. We fumble with clothing as we stumble to her bedroom, forgetting about lights or sounds or anything else; it's momentum.

She unbuckles my belt, pulls me closer, leans down and hovers over my waist before pulling my jeans down. I roll my shoulders back and take off my shirt. I stand there for a minute before I pull her up to me, touch her face, bury my head in her neck and take her in.

I throw her onto the bed and crawl on top of her, my hands roaming her body. I push my weight onto her so she can feel me. I hear her moan beneath, wrap her legs around me. I take her thighs and open her up.

*   *   *

"Is this what you imagined it would be?" she asks me late one evening after we've been on the phone awhile. She's been coming to Eton the weekends; I've been driving to Atlanta to have dinner with her in the middle of the week after she gets done at the club. We take turns cooking.

I think about my answer for a while. "I could never have come close to imagining this," I tell her, and it's true. "When you have lived your whole life in the dark, you don't even know what light is."

She gets quiet on the other end of the line, but I can hear her breathing.

"Well said," she says and laughs. "You surprise me all of the time, Carmine, you really do."

"I surprise myself, too." I tell her about all the things Ma and I have been up to around the house and how we've been sharing these big, potluck meals, how I've been taking walks with her in the morning, trying to keep her energy levels up. I tell her that I got a repair book from the library and how I've been making upgrades to the old beast of a truck, new spark plugs and engine mounts, even a bed liner. I tell her about the time I took Ma dress shopping, the awkward moment in the lingerie section, how I wasn't able to change the hot water heater at the house, but that at least I was able to find it.

But I don't tell her that at night I still think I hear Pa's screams reverberate through the house, how I still feel the itch in my feet to run, how I watch the stock market, count my money, apply for jobs overseas, that I still cringe when I pass the "Welcome to Eton" sign on the way to the grocery store.

*   *   *

When I step out of the church just before dusk, the sky is a purple pink and it stretches from end to end, as far as I can see, and I feel light on my feet. I've gone to see Pastor Stanley again. Some of the basics are still so hard, turning wrong into right, traveling new paths when the grooves in the brain call to others. I keep thinking of Pa's body in the ground, and it sends waves of panic through me. Being with Z takes so much presence. Sometimes it's a real struggle just to be willing.

"It's a choice you make every moment, Carmine; it's that simple. Continue to choose love and peace, and love and peace is what you will have. But it's not always gonna be easy." He's grown a mustache, and his bald head still shines. We drink coffee in paper cups and nibble on day-old muffins.

"Yes, but why can't it be easy? Why do things have to be so hard?" I look at him pleadingly. "It was so much easier to be a bastard than to do the right thing," I say.

"We make it hard; it is supposed to be easy. We imagine fear instead of love because we think we're so vulnerable. Essentially, it's a lack of faith in ourselves, in the world, in God."

"But we *are* vulnerable, aren't we? I've felt that way my whole life." I look at him for a long time. His eyes are black and wet, but so full of peace.

"Let the fear go, let the guilt go, and you'll be free," he tells me.

Chapter 18

An hour later, I walk toward the old railroad tracks slowly. I wind up and down streets I don't remember much about; I look at the old ridges of the mountains to the east; I go toward my future. I run Pastor Stanley's words over in my head; I want to know peace, and this has always been in the way.

I hear him again and again as I walk the path toward Eric's house; I remember his name, his family from the day's gray newspaper. I see his face when I look up and see the remains of the old dilapidated warehouse; it leans and has holes in it, the aluminum thinning, even the old silver light poles lean.

I sit on the curb, and my mind wanders back to that inky night, the humidity in the air, the cool breeze that stretched down from the ridges of these mountains, the locusts—they were singing, it was late July.

It's hard to imagine myself as ever being a child, soft elbows, lilted voice, spitting tobacco into old Campbell's soup cans. It all must have been a movie I saw once, even the hard calluses on Pa's hands, Ma's soft cry, all set against a fake Gulf of Mexico, so easy to imagine that none of it was true.

A school bus stops a block up the road and some black children step off. I see their school uniforms, white shirts and khaki pants and braids moving on top of their heads as they walk; there's a chatter among them, a vibration. They spot me sitting on the curb and slow their paces.

I stand up and run my eyes over the silver of the new tracks lining the road across the street, hear the whistle of an oncoming train, turn around and search the house numbers to be sure I'm at the right place.

I look down and my shoes are untied. I clear my throat for fear that my voice will squeak like it did then.

I run a few words around in my head. Tap my foot with each syllable, practice the inflections. "I saw your boy get killed. I didn't try to stop it. I am sorry." It has to be simpler than that. It's too much. I feel like that heavy rock is in my hand instead of theirs, that I'm using it to gouge his head, think his mother will spill out onto the sidewalk and blame me for it all anyway.

I think all of this so silly and unnecessary, and I start to turn around. These old wounds are just that, old and stagnant. What can be the benefit of opening them up? Can't peace still get in?

The kids from the bus get closer to me and then stop; their chatter takes on a heavier tone. They're young, almost teenagers, but not quite. The sun is in the middle of the sky and it leans down heavily; they look at me, smile, some glare and then look away. I study their round bodies, remember my gangly limbs, search their faces for what I might mean to them.

"I'm sorry," I yell to them. "Some of us are like me, like I was, but not all; we just don't know any better, we don't know anything." They look at me strangely, but a second longer than they want to.

I lean down to tie my shoes and they walk past me. I zip up my jacket and jingle the change in my pocket. If this is the right thing, why does it feel so bad?

I turn around and walk two doors down to 301. The house is quiet. The welcome mat has hummingbirds on it and says, "Life is short so come on in and stay awhile." On the porch, an old swing sways with the wind, a plant hangs from the two posts holding the porch roof up; inside, a TV vibrates.

I pull open the tattered screen door and knock on the wooden door softly; there are three small windows on it, but I don't look in. When I hear footsteps shuffling across the floor, I hold my breath and wait.

She's wearing small pearl earrings, her hair has grayed, but her skin and face are just as smooth as nearly twenty years ago. I remember seeing her through the school bus window, at school functions; sometimes we'd see her at the grocery store. Her body is soft and round, and her voice is so tender, so tender, I shake. She sounds like Eton.

"Can I help you?" She puts her hand on her hip and looks at me hard. She reminds me of my own ma; they are close to the same age, I don't hear anyone in the house, and I wonder if she's alone. A TV blares a familiar talk show host's voice, laughing and jeering; I can see why people watch.

"Hello. Are you Mrs. Clemsy?" I shift on my feet, try to push everything but this moment out of my mind.

She nods and pushes a straight pin back in her hair at the nape of her neck. "Yes, I am. What can I do for you?"

"Ma'am, you don't know me, and I should have come a long time ago, but I know what happened to your son."

Her face changes. The shallow lines grow deeper and darker; her eyebrows turn in. She takes a deep breath but doesn't say anything, holds a lot in, her lips pursed. The TV in the background grows louder when a laundry detergent commercial comes on. A school bus passes in front of the house with a big whoosh.

I step out of the present for a moment, back then, to that night, how I considered stepping in front of that train, its sea of light like what the gates of heaven must be like. I can even feel the old rock-band shirt I was wearing, its soft cotton sticking to my chest.

"Ma'am, I just wanted to . . . I came here to . . . see, I've been living my whole life with this. I've been tortured by it, same as you, and I've got to be free, and I thought if I could set you free and be free and I could come here and tell you the truth finally and ask your forgiveness and it could be better and . . ."

She straightens up her body, and her words come out heavy and firm.

"Now you listen here, son. You got something to tell me about my boy, you say it and you say it now. Otherwise you get off my porch right now." Little beads of sweat form on her forehead. She pushes the screen door open and steps out onto the porch, stands close to me.

I don't turn around, but I can hear the kids behind me, the scuffs of their tennis shoes on the pavement, their chatter about what this white man is doing here and what he come to say and why he's bothering old Mrs. Clemsy. I hear the toy phones open and close, bubble gum pop on their lips; in the periphery I see a young man smooth the hair on his head.

"I saw them do it, me, ma'am; I saw them kill him. I sat there across from those tracks and I watched them do it. I never said a thing, didn't try to stop them . . . It was some kids from school that did it, ma'am, just a bunch of kids from Eton High messing around and it was wrong, and I . . ."

The world goes black when I feel the sting of her hand on my cheek. I feel the bottom of the door hit the tips of my boots and push me back. I stagger a few feet, stunned, fall to the bottom of the stairs.

I open my eyes a few seconds later, and she hovers above me.

"Why this? Why now?" she asks me, her chest rising and falling.

I stand up a few feet from her, hear that old train in the distance; it sounds the same. I want to feel its wind rush past me again.

"I should have come to you back then; I should have tried to help him . . ." I wave my hands in front of me, as though I'm holding two white flags. I look at her pleadingly.

"I know who you are. You and your family ain't never done any good in these parts." She turns away and starts walking up the stairs.

I go to the end of the stairs and stare up at her. She stands on her porch, hands on her hips.

"My boy's been dead a long time, a long time. The police never did spend any time with it. Besides, there weren't no mystery to it anyway. Everyone knew how it went down. You should not have come here." She wipes something invisible on the apron she's wearing, looks up the street. The sun climbs behind the clouds and the air is cooler.

"Ma'am, I haven't done much right with my life; I've caused a lot of hurt, but nothing was worse than what I did that night, turning the other cheek. And I'm sorry, ma'am, very sorry for that. That's why I came. Your boy deserved better than that."

She sighs deep, circles her neck a little; her body falls into the porch a little. She looks at me for a long time, as though waiting for the real truth to fall from my lips.

"You should have helped my boy, God, should you have helped him . . ." She starts to cry, holds back, uses the apron to wipe her eyes.

"But the past is already gone, and there's nothing we can do about that." She straightens, stands up tall, points her finger at me.

"So, you, you get on out of here." She doesn't blink once as she says it, an older anger rising up in her cheeks. "I mean it," she says.

I look at her for a second longer and then turn the other way. I walk two blocks down the road before turning around one last time. She's still standing there, looking my way. I wave a little, shove my hands in my pockets, and walk on home. It's the best I could do.

Chapter 19

FOR THE NEXT FEW weeks, time seems to take on a mind of its own—swirling in and out, stopping at times, moving forward at a speed I've never known, quietly and pervasively rearranging things in my life: relationships, eating habits, even hygiene, the state of my dreams changing all the while. In a way I had to become a boy again and start over, little by little, reconstructing the mountains in my mind, the immovable structures that kept me hard and unreachable and so goddamn heavy it felt as though I couldn't move myself during some of those years in Dallas.

I'd never really been with anyone my whole life, never really honored or revered a person; everything began and ended with me, with what I had to prove, or the thing I felt I needed to forget. It was all new territory to me.

"Baby, just let me in," sometimes she'd plead with me, circling her long arms around me, the smell of her skin like pumpkin pie and lilacs. I melted and all the lines blurred within me. I didn't breathe for fear of dislodging a single sensation.

"Z, I'm here, I'm here. It's just that I don't know if I can . . ." And then I would need to flee; I'd leave the room or jump in the truck and drive. Other times, I was better, brave; other times I leaned into the fear, the same way you have to lean into the turn when your car is spinning out of control, the white ice beneath it turning it in circles, I was afraid of the slipperiness of love.

Sometimes I'd ask her opinion on things like God or politics, and it always came back to color and the way the world is melting together, slowly, she says.

When I got home that night, I finally told her about Eric. She was part of the reason I'd found the courage to do it, to try to make something right come from such a wrong past. I wanted to have a real chance with her, and I couldn't let the weight of my guilt hold us down, keep me from her.

"I've lived with it my whole life, Z. And now I'm here with you, and it ain't right. I wanted that woman to know how sorry I've been, how I've carried that weight, how often I'd wished it'd been different, that I'd' been different. I want you to know that, Z." I'm sitting on the steps of my porch; she stands in front of me, and I can see a sliver of the moon behind her, hear the trees push with the wind.

She looks at me for so long, and I'm not sure if she will turn and walk away. I wouldn't blame her if she did. I stop breathing, wait, feel a sense of relief and fear all at the same time; the rest is out of my hands.

"I've been dealing with this stuff my whole life, Carmine, my whole life. It ain't a season to be black, Carmine; it's a life, and in these parts you get used to watching your back and you get used to people's ignorance, you get used to getting less."

Her voice reminds me of the way it sounded at the club that first night, sharp and jagged. I think I've lost her.

"I understand, Z." I stand up, start to walk toward her.

"No, you don't understand, Carmine, you don't understand at all."

I try to put my arms around her, but she pushes me away. I sit back down on the steps of the porch. I can hear Ma shuffling around in the house; a few of the floorboards creak, and I can smell the dryer tumbling.

I think about the morning at the table with Pa, how he excused it all so easily, a person dying because of his skin color. I wince as I remember the KKK rallies in the town center and how I watched his brown skin turn gray in the mildewed air of that building. If you ain't part of the solution, you're part of the problem, I can hear Diego saying.

She rubs her face with her hands, smooths her hair, taps her feet, and then lets out a long sigh. "But it's not your fault."

Her shoulders turn in a bit. She walks up the steps and sits down beside me. It is so quiet now I think I can hear her heart beating.

"I'm sorry, Z. I hate that part of me." I slide my hand into hers, hold it tight. "It ain't right."

"You did the right thing, you did the right thing by going to her. It doesn't make any difference, but it was right." She squeezes my hand.

"I want the world to be different for my children," she says. "But change doesn't come easily, especially not in the backwoods on these old clay roads." She smiles, crosses her legs, and stretches them out.

"But it has changed, Z, it has, and it will continue to." I desperately wanted to believe this.

There were only a handful of black people on one side of town and there was the side of town where the old whites lived, and our house was somewhere in between. A place with more fresh air than you could breathe, with dark and foreboding mountains full of life, in the pocket of earth, something else.

People looked at us, people watched the sun set in the hills beyond us, and we kept our eyes there. On the thing that was bigger than us, on the thing that we were trying to be, to unite with. But it wasn't always easy.

People made comments and my fists would tense as I searched the crowd for a face belonging to those words. I wanted to fight. To hurt. To beg Z to talk to them about all the colors, about our brown world, all the things she knew so well. It was hard to keep believing in a world that said love wasn't true.

"Baby. This is us. It's not them. We've got nothing to justify. Don't make it about them." I look into the darkness of her brown eyes and understand immediately what she means. I had spent my life living by the demands of my ego. I relaxed. Walked with her. We grew.

We tried to spend time in Atlanta, to make plans, to live her life and then mine, to be in a place where we could be swallowed up for a while, where changes are less noticeable, contrast is expected and appreciated and glossed, and life rushes on with a pace that is like a soft hum and everyone spins the kaleidoscope. Atlanta is a reflection of many things.

I liked being in the city, but I couldn't stay away for long; I worried about Ma. In my mind, I could see the darkness and the loneliness erasing her when the pencil lines were just starting to be noticeable. I'd drive back to Eton, take her to lunch, walk her around the block, talk to her, reflect herself back to her so that she could see life.

Sometimes she put on lipstick and began to transform. Sometimes she showed me pictures of herself as a girl. Sometimes she asked Z about music. Other times, she bled out, said she didn't know how much longer she'd be around, smoked more cigarettes, refilled a flask, walked from room to room with one of Pa's old shirts.

"Carmine, everyone is dead, you know." She was sweeping the kitchen floor slowly, and her new yellow dress brushed her knees and I wondered if she could feel it as I could see it. Everything, for me, had become about color and about sensation. I could hear the car alarm five blocks away, feel the hum of the train at the station on the other side of town; life had given me powers, life had become something else.

"We're not all dead, Ma, and neither are you."

She stopped sweeping and looked at me for a long time. I watched her every movement and realized I still wanted the thing I'd always wanted: her love. She put the broom in the closet and went back to her chair, but she didn't light a cigarette and she didn't take a drink.

Z became the center of our solar system, and the two of us orbited around her. We all wanted something to do. Z had her own hills to traverse, a journey to navigate, somewhere to go herself.

"Mama never really did anything, but she was always so busy." Z rests her thumbs in the belt loops of her jeans as we walk the streets of downtown Eton at dark, and sometimes right before breakfast. Storefront windows glow or stand still, little stores for everything: shoes, books, greeting cards, even a store with just rope.

"I adored her, wanted nothing but to be close to her, but she always seemed so temporary to me. She was never in one place very long. Mama, Daddy, if they stood or sat in a room for longer than five minutes, it was a holiday or some other ritual; it never quite came together." A smile forms at the edges of her lips and her eyes reach for something far away, something she can't yet see.

"Daddy's skin was so black. So dark. Like coal. Mama's was lighter. Like sandpaper. These nuances are very important to black people, Carmine, did you know that?" She grabs my hand and we keep walking.

"Your mama doesn't seem to like me, Carmine, but I know it's not because I'm black." She laughs as she says this and then pulls me into an ice cream shop.

We took turns being the navigator, leading the way. I opened the shed door without going in and closed it; she began to paint and then folded up the canvas and threw it away. We wanted movement, but we were afraid of it, too.

Her stories continued. "We wore elaborate clothes. Everything had a meaning. Our slippers. Our names. We built our life around these underlying meanings; so did our neighbors. It was our identity. But I could never find anything original in myself, and that troubled me deeply." She sighs so deeply I think she might collapse.

CHAPTER 20

IT'S A WARM TUESDAY when I decide to open Pa's work shed and let the light in.

The insides of it are dusty and stale, full of broken pieces, sharp corners, furniture so close to being completed. There's a half-completed bench and an armchair done but without the arms. I can feel the wood shavings beneath my feet and smell the sawdust in the air, and it's so different from the balmy and translucent light of a high-rise office building.

I sit on the bench near the worktable and pick up a rusted saw, run my fingers over its teeth, feel the cold metal on my fingers. Ma tells me how Pa always dreamed of having a real studio somewhere, with new and shiny tools, lots of space to spread out.

I sit on the bench for a long time looking around, watching how the dust particles float in the air, realizing they are the same ones that floated around Pa as he worked, and that he wasn't an ending and I am not a beginning.

I see a small piece of carved wood on top of a pile of raw cypress. It is a horse, small, with muscular legs and a long back, so intricately carved and smoothed, so solid. I hold it in my hands for a long time and run my fingers over it; in my fingers it feels warm.

I look into the pile and there are other carvings: a small plane, a tiny baseball bat, even an intricate train with wheels on the caboose and windows and pipes coming from it. I imagine Pa, old Ron, chiseling and smoothing and working until his fingers ached, while I was in the house aching for him, longing for his tenderness, understanding, something softer than the back of his hand, the sting of his words.

I walk out of the workshop, horse in hand, and slam the door behind me. I want to leave it all behind, but I don't know if I can.

*   *   *

I am in the tavern again, with a beer and a shot, the horse warm in my pocket. The smell of old cigarettes and sweat and dark corners smells foreign and rotten, but it's a cocoon, warm and cradling, and I enter it again, its shape molding to me like it has always done.

I've been sober a few weeks now, trying like hell to stay present and to watch and feel what love brings, what commitment asks of you, to be something that I always knew I could be. It's so much easier in theory than in practice. But I don't understand it, the way it was, the way it feels now, why it keeps coming back. That old me just won't die.

My skin feels like it's crawling, like my insides are trying to climb right out from within me. I order a third shot of Patron and wait. The back of my mind is filled with red, and my fists open and close.

There's a small window at the end of the bar, and I watch the day turn into evening, then into night. I keep slamming drinks, and inside I feel like choking and hurting someone, but I don't. I just want to know where he ends and where I begin and what one has to do with the other.

* * *

A few hours later I am walking down the alley, and I hear that little horse in my pocket saying, "She loves you, Carmine, she really loves you." I take it out of my pocket and look at it one last time before I throw it in the dumpster and walk away.

I walk through the dark streets of Eton right along the railroad tracks, and I watch the stars up above move in and out of the sky while I am still. I kick rocks down the block, and it is so quiet I can hear each one until it hits the curb and stops completely. In the distance that old train whistle howls. I walk toward the edge of town, to meet the tracks; I want to stare the eye down again.

I pull out my cell phone and dial Z's number and hang up. I dial home and hang up too. I don't know if I can be anyone's man or son or if I can be anything other than what I've always been.

*   *   *

The phone rings, and I hear Melanie pick it up. I can't remember a whole lot from the night before, but I remember Melanie showing up at the door, and the bottle of wine and pretty little things in her suitcase and the softness of her short skirt and then the back roads of Eton, the feel of the old truck's interior, her sweating on top of me.

"Hello?" Her voice is smoky and naked. I know it's Z on the phone. I wake up from a light sleep and stretch my legs, my pupils dilate and I hold my breath. I am trying to remember the day, the week, the contours of my life, where it's been and what this moment means, the blonde, the me, the scope, the hills, and the consequences.

She rolls over and hands me the phone. I am unshaven and hungover, full awake, but I don't grab the receiver. I lean over the bed and remember the dream I was just having where I am a superhero flying above Eton; I'm wearing a cape, and my special power is that I can tell the truth, see the future.

I am wearing my old gym shorts, the ones I wore way back in Port Arthur; and in the dream I have the angst and the buckteeth and the burning desire to be something else, but I am smiling so much that my mouth is dry and I can hear Ma laughing somewhere in the clouds and I swoop in and save the day every day.

I hear Mel laugh then speak into the phone. It's what she does, without knowing how or why. She is trouble.

She thinks nothing of it, women, there's always been women, a collage of them streaming in and out of my past, my future. She's known me for years but she makes no claims to me. She's troubled not in the least but knows the caller must be.

"Honey, I am just an old friend of Carmine's. He'll call you back. Okay?"

"Did someone call earlier?" I ask uncertain, but somewhere in the back of my mind, I feel Z, a distance, a brush of cold air, a missing piece. Melanie laughs again; this too, familiar.

"Yes baby. I think she said her name was Zee. Does that sound familiar to you?" She's only half-kidding. She knows, too; the same way Z does but differently.

I jump out of bed. The drunk from last night has worn off in a single instant. I'm naked and my limp cock bounces in the air and takes a short moment to settle before I speak. I look down at it briefly; the way I might make eye contact with someone when they enter the room.

"Oh my God. What'd you say to her?" I've never been so afraid in my life. Again, I'm the kid on the 3-point line; the court is dangerously silent behind me.

"Shit, Carmine, I didn't say anything." She's still lying in bed, but now she's smoking a cigarette. Her left breast has snuck out of her nightgown and suddenly it looks stale and indigestible. I look at my penis again and wonder what we ever saw in her.

"I'm not kidding, Melanie. What did you tell her?" I'm pacing the room now, completely butt-naked, nervous, on the edge of enraged. I look at her for a long time and see her the way I would have from my bike, as a teenager, and I think *gross, she's old and she looks cheap and she smokes . . .* I don't know what to do with her or the me that is here in this room.

I feel like a block of stone and look at her for a long time. I smirk. Shake my head. Tell her to go back home, watch as she picks up her clothes, scattered around the room, rubs the old mascara from her eyes. It's like another scene of my former life run over again and again.

"Carmine . . ." she starts to say, looks at me for a long time, her eyes begin to pool, but she rubs them and pushes the emotion away.

"You know where to find me." She smiles lightly, without emotion this time, as though this doesn't mean anything, as though she was already on her way out. I wait and listen for the front door to close behind her. I can't help but think she somehow likes these terms, this way of coming and going, being pushed out the door when real life needs to take over.

I grab the phone and call Z. While it rings, I walk around looking for Ma, try to feel her energy in the house, needing, wanting something to be the same, there and reliable. She is not home, and I try to remember if she was there when we came in the night before. Sometimes she sips one small glass of whiskey the whole night long, refilling it with ice as the hours pass, never going to sleep; other times she slips into bed by early evening, not to be seen until late the next morning.

Z's machine picks up. It feels cold on the other end of the line.

"Z, please pick up. I need to talk to you. See . . . I just . . . I don't know . . . it's just . . . Anyway, please pick up, please call me, something. I'll explain everything. I promise."

I am the adolescent boy again, pleading with my father to understand why I'd stolen the pack of cigarettes. The harsh buckle of the black belt is near me, and my legs are short and I can't run fast enough and there's nothing I can do to get away from what is.

I brew a pot of coffee in the old percolator and sit on the corner of my bed. The Eton light is trying to sneak through the blinds of the room, but I pull the big drapes closed and refuse to look out.

The next thing I know, I am at the Atlanta airport standing in front of the Continental Airlines kiosk, swiping my credit card for a flight to DFW airport. All I know is that I have to get back on solid ground.

*   *   *

On the plane, I imagine how my updated resume will look on white weighted paper, how Ma will have the best of semiretirement homes, how Z will find the black man of her dreams.

I can feel my new self crawling back into the folds of my old skin, and it feels good. I step off the plane and leave Eton behind.

"Cabby, take me to the Sky Bar now. I've got some celebrating to do!" I laugh out loud, the way I would have six months ago, and lean back into the vinyl seat. I drift off into a meditative state and try not to think. But I do. I think of the Carmichael account for the first time in months, about that cat Carmine that used to be me, the man I want to be again. I place myself back into the role: clean, cold, well-dressed, calculated, in control; I don't owe anyone anything.

I know I could easily find a new firm to work for, even if it wasn't advertising, a new ladder to climb. I know there are always women to monopolize and drinks to chill and money to be made, and that unlike God or health or Christmas, they would always be there, waiting and willing, and you don't have to give them any notice or promise them any love. I tried to change, for a minute or two, I thought I was actually capable of being that good guy, fair and honest, something like light, hanging in there like the rest. But I was wrong.

The Sky Bar is as loud and as welcoming as I remember. The club music thumps and the Thursday night crowd sways and moves, and I manage to get a place at the bar by the dance floor. It is worlds away from the Shack with its expensive lighting and high-priced drinks and marble and manicured skin, and I take it all in. I drink another martini and watch a woman on the dance floor closely. Her skin looks pasty and clean, her shape young but solid, twists and soft curves and an empty mind; I want to taste her. I watch her as if she is my prey, but my concentration is off; images keep floating into the scope of my vision: Pa's thin body, Z's jeans, Ma's hands on my shoulder, the leather of the Bible at the Baptist church, Pastor Stanley's shiny head. I look at the veins in my hand and try to get control of my thoughts, to find my lines, to step into my old role. I know I can.

I order another drink and move in closer. I want to be that guy again—ruthless, easy, removed. I want to go back, to rewind. I want to hunt, be hunted, to gather and to hoard, to not know again, the way it once was, me apart.

I drink two more martinis before finding my way to the back side of her, the deep bass of the music under my feet, her hair on my face. My hand finds her back, its polyester dress, the bumps of her spine. She turns around.

"Hey," she whispers into my ear.

I can smell the alcohol on her as if I've never had a drop of it in my life.

"I'm Carmine." I say it directly into her ear so she gets it, feels me; my eyes dilate and my blood moves faster.

"I know," she says. "I know exactly who you are." She's still smiling and closes the space between us. I feel her hands on my lower back, and she begins to move me and breathe into me. I can feel the martinis swirl around my head, the jet lag in my feet. Somewhere in the distance, I think I hear thunder. For a second, I think I am him again: I move like him and I sound like him when I speak and in my hands, she feels like the others did, but I am not him anymore. I am not him. I stop moving and look at her for a long time.

"What's wrong?" She keeps her hands on my waist and smiles.

"I don't know," I tell her and walk away. I take my place at the bar again. I sit there until closing time, waiting for the answer, waiting for the fog to lift, waiting to know something.

*   *   *

The Dallas skyline looks like I remember it: cold and docile in the day, piercing in some spots, and so big, stretching farther than my reach is these days. When I wake up in my penthouse the next day, I feel overwhelmed by the vibrations.

I look out onto the ledge, to the night that it almost ended for me. I think back to the curve in the road, the scalding hot hours watching Pa die, the screeching of Ma's grief, and losing the Carmichael account seems like one of those problems on sitcoms that can be fixed with a hug. I don't know what problems are anymore, or how to distinguish them from the folds of life; they just are. Everything feels like warm liquid around me.

I remember the girl at the club and the sour in my stomach when she moved close to me, acknowledged my reputation, claimed to know me.

I think about Z, the weeks we've spent together, the future we've talked about, the way I've learned to care for my mother. I can't believe that any of it is really true, that I actually had any of it in me.

I can smell the newness in the air, the gleam, the anesthesia of my former self; the penthouse is a prop, I see that now.

Ma's message is still on the answering machine. The light blinks red, on and off, and I want it to turn off forever; I want to let go. I listen to Ma's voice on the machine and hear Pa in the background again, feel the red energy rise up within and twist my stomach, and then watch it go.

I remember a slogan I once wrote: "Start where you are."

CHAPTER 21

A COUPLE OF DAYS later, I am packing up the penthouse and deciding what to do with it all: the stainless steel pots and pans and the down linens and the expensive silk shirts and leather shoes and closets full of things with tags still on them. I remember buying these things, coveting them and using them to prove I was better than what I'd come from, using my money as insulation. I lean on the steel refrigerator and think about calling Ma.

I can hear the Dallas traffic below me, humming and rushing, so different from the sounds and hills of Georgia, the crickets and gushing of breezes, everything so quiet and green. I find my old briefcase on the kitchen table and throw it in the trash can. I remember the paperwork that still needs taken care of for Pa, life insurance and deeds and financials; it all seems insignificant. I think about the word *son*, and it still feels bittersweet in my mouth.

There's a knock at the door, and before I answer, I know who it is. She's followed me for years like a stray puppy, waiting for me to drop her a crumb, a used bone with no meat; I've led her astray for so long.

When I open the door, there she stands with the same look on her face she had in my room in Eton a few days ago, innocent and hurt and pointed; she's always had her own agenda too. For the first time, I see that she's just a girl.

"Melanie. Listen . . ." My words drop to the floor. I don't know where to start or if I should begin to explain something I don't yet fully understand. I am not positive I can even form real words. I've sat alone for days now.

I try again. We both knew she didn't have the power to hold me, that there wasn't enough space for her anywhere here.

"I'm going to stay in Georgia for good," I say, surprised that I've said it aloud, my decision finally making itself known.

"Yes, Carmine, I know. It's that girl, isn't it?" Her back is to me; I think of reaching for her again. I sit down on my bed we have had sex in at least a hundred times over the past ten years. She sits down on the other side, her back still toward me, the curves of her body so tender and seductive, I want to dominate her like I always have, maybe even fall in love with her. The impulses seem to come out of nowhere. I watch them. The blinds are up and the afternoon sun stretches across the bed in shaded lines. It's the sun of endings, the sun of growth and change, the sun of hurt—it's all the same energy.

"I always thought you cared about me. I knew it wasn't a lot, but I thought it would turn into more . . . eventually." She doesn't cry, it's not her way, but she opens and closes her legs and bends her head toward me as she talks.

"That morning, when I realized how you felt about that woman, when I saw it in your eyes, I suddenly knew the difference between what you'd given me and the things you felt for her. Was it respect? Was it love? I don't know. But it was a breaking point for me, Carmine. An epiphany even. And I felt so ridiculous for coming to Eton, for hunting you down like a piece of meat, because even before I got on that plane, I knew you didn't want me."

She continues speaking, and her voice sounds slippery and wet. "That's part of the reason I'm here today. These things I'm picking up, they're only fragments of a picture I was trying to paint, the way I wanted things to be for us, for myself. I just always felt that if somehow I could get you to love me, I'd be complete, I'd be valuable." She gets up and walks toward the bathroom.

"I feel like a fool, Carmine, for loving you at all, because you don't know how to love anyone." She slams the bathroom door behind her.

I walk to the bathroom door and rest my hand on the doorknob. I remember being here before, last year sometime, this same look on my face. This same time of day. She'd come over for those same earrings and toothbrush, this time for good, she'd said.

"Mel, can you come out of there?" I sit down on the side of the bed and wait for her. I feel like I owe her something. I feel like I need to prove something to myself, to the world, to some power larger than myself.

"I need to know that you loved me in your own way. I need to know that the last ten years of my life weren't wasted. I never asked you for anything, but . . ." She stops and stares at me.

"Yes, Melanie, I have loved you. I never said it, but I did. It's true. And I'm sorry." I take her hands in mine and pull her close to me, place my arms around her legs. We stay there for a few minutes before she pulls away and I watch her gather her things.

"I guess this is finally good-bye," she says and smiles, the look on her face open and resolute, her shoes in her hand. I hear her feet shuffle through the apartment; the door closes softly behind her.

I sit with the understanding that most men both love and hate and like them, I will spend a lifetime trying to weigh the balance in the love direction, trying to see what is real, not just the truth of my hurts or the hope of my desires.

I hadn't imagined that my Pa had anything on the other side of his hate or his righteousness but I believe, probably, too, it was easier for me to believe this. Hate is cold but it is comfortable. If my life and my father's death has taught me anything, it is that it is by far the hardest human endeavor to just sit still and be loved, to be open and willing to believe in it, to hold it as yours, and to accept the inevitability of the human smudge that sometimes covers that basic love in us all. My father was rotten in many ways and he left marks on my skin and in my heart and twisted and turned my mother, too, in ways that she'll never fully recover from, but he loved us. I can't go back and move things around, like furniture in an old room, I've just got to accept the way things are. In time, they may change in my mind, but they may not.

* * *

The drive back to Georgia is a long one. I stare out the window to the road for hours at a time and watch the landscapes of the country pass me by: the hues of white, brown, a series of reds in leaves in fields, on flowers, and in people. There are so many colors everywhere. I stop at filling stations in West Texas, Oklahoma, Arkansas. I see faces in all different shades of brown, think of Z.

In my rearview mirror, I see the contents of my past in the backseat: two big leather suitcases full of clothes and a few mementos from the high life, my old Bible, some shoes, a box full of old greeting cards from Ma. I've lived nearly fifteen years of life in the sky, and the only things with meaning can be stuffed inside two leather squares.

Outside my window I count the rows of green plants and hum songs in my head. Sometimes my right knee begins to shake, but I take another cup of coffee and let it pass. I don't want to drink at every corner, at every sign of trouble anymore. I want to know I can be and live deeper than that.

The hum of the engine satisfies my mind mostly, but I still pick up my cell phone to call her many times, only to put it down again. I don't know what to say or if I can fight for her, or if there is space in the middle where we can meet.

I run into rainstorms at the border of Georgia. The luminous mountains ahead of me, the gray pavement below, my wipers try to keep up with the work. My ankle feels numb from the hours of push, but I am ready to go over the edge and into another land, so different from the past, one without my pa, one without the guilt of a kid who was just doing what he was taught.

I stop at a gas station to fill up, pick up my phone to try her again. I look at my watch, imagine she's in Atlanta back on that tattered stage again, giving herself away. I cringe, spot the pay phone across the street.

She doesn't know it's me right away, doesn't recognize the number on her phone. I speak, my breathing heavy and weighted. I shiver, my face still so wet from the rain, dripping almost; large raindrops hang from the tip of my nose, my eyelashes, even my chin.

"Zaire.

"Listen.

"The thought of you being gone from my life makes me feel like my chest's going to give in. It's that simple.

"Tell me you don't feel anything, and I'll leave you alone forever." I listen, bright-eyed; the rest of my life waits in the wings.

"We made no promises, and that's all we've got. Nothing!" Her voice is so weighted when she says it, I can hear her heavy breathing on the other end of the line.

"But I should have promised you, Zaire. You're all there is. I am tired of living in a shadow with open-ended questions."

My T-shirt sticks to my chest and I shiver.

"I was the child who rescued raccoons and nursed them back to health. I've been mad for years; all I know is that this anger must be something good that's iced up." I am not sure if she's there, but I can still hear the club's music far in the background.

"See the problem with the St. Clairs is that we handle ourselves too well. You'll never catch us unsteady on our feet. From the time I learned to crawl, we'd tiptoe past each other. Then we'd curl miserably under our sheets, me sobbing, not from what we'd said, but from things we didn't say. No goodnight kisses, no hugs, just thick air that you could cut with a chain saw.

I'm speaking not for her anymore, but for me. The years of therapy never scheduled, the boyhood angst never articulated, the male insecurities never made whole.

"Everywhere I look, I hear people hurt from this so-called love. But I finally know it doesn't have to be that way. Promise me you'll stay with me? I promise you, the past is finally past."

I wipe the rain from my face and hold the phone tight. I can hear her breathing again.

"I want to believe that, Carmine, I really do."

She hangs up, and I hold onto the phone for a while before walking back to the car. A few hours later, I am back in my old bed, my belly full, the past finally off my chest.

*   *   *

I show up in Atlanta at her house the next morning with an umbrella. When she opens the door, she just stands there for a long time looking at me. At first, her eyes hold anger in them, simmering just behind the pupils, but she then softens, her shoulders falling; she shifts her weight from foot to foot. She stands there for a long time like this, not letting me in, not moving, staring at something behind me.

"Baby, I'm glad you're back," she finally tells me and walks me into her apartment. We hold hands for a long time on the sofa before I begin to talk. I tell her how I had to learn to forgive my pa, to understand that he was imperfect, that I'm imperfect, to learn to accept that he loved me, too, so that I can somehow become whole myself, so that I can learn to believe in love, to trust it. She tells me of her own struggles with her own father and mother, how her father was so perfect in her eyes, but that after his death, she'd realized, too, that he was just a man, with sins and indecision, and that understanding had helped her be just a girl, too, sometimes soft, sometimes hard, but always acceptable.

She stops speaking rather suddenly. Her head is resting on my shoulder and I think maybe she's fallen asleep or something, but then I hear her breathe in very deeply, as though filling a balloon.

"Carmine. I'm pregnant. We are pregnant." She's leaning up now, looking at me, at my unshaven face and misty eyes, and we stay that way for a long time. It takes awhile for what she's just said to sink in, but when it does, I want to scream.

"Oh my god, I can't believe it. I can't believe it." I want to say more about how wonderful our life will be, how great a father I'll become, how I'll never mess up, but words aren't much use most of the time, I've got to show her.

For the rest of the afternoon, we talk about the things that have brought us here, the things we've shared, how Rumi was right about finding that space out where right and wrong don't exist. I don't know how I've been forgiven, I don't know why I've been given so many second chances, but I'm finally gonna do this thing right.

CHAPTER 22

WE NEVER REALLY CONSCIOUSLY decided to get married. We never had the talk and we never went ring shopping and we never lay awake into the dark of night talking about it. These things, we agreed, seemed superficial. Either it was or it wasn't—we didn't need to prove it on the outside and we didn't need a ceremony to say it was so.

But one morning, I decide I need to make it official, for tradition's sake, to give us a day to talk about forever, to give her a story.

We've just woken up. It is just after eight and I am headed to the shop. We've grown into a familiar routine. She wakes up at six, for her run, coffee at the window; I stagger into the kitchen sometime later for coffee, breakfast right away, and the morning news. It has been six months, but every single morning I get up, I want to run to that kitchen because I know she'll be there. Waiting. I never grow tired of looking at that skin, wishing it were over mine, touching those lips, wishing I could climb inside, and listening to her talk.

I never had those boyhood fantasies of proposals, no recollections of those in chick flicks or on corny sitcoms; I had nothing to go on but the truth of the matter.

We're standing there in the kitchen. She's chewing on a pear. I'm grabbing the half-and-half out of the fridge.

"Z, I think we should get married." I pause, just long enough for her to see the uncertainty in my eyes. I still wonder if she'll say yes, still can't take any of it for granted, for fear that I'll wake up with it all gone.

It came together just as simply; she was right there with me, like always, her gaze on something bigger than us both. "I think so, too."

In the kitchen, the fridge still hanging open, we hug each other. The early morning sun reaches in and touches both of our shoulders. I sit her up on the kitchen island of our new house, and she holds me between her legs. We stay that way for as long as we can stand it.

* * *

We plan the wedding, our official union, quite casually, and laugh about it, the logistics of what needs to be done and how and when.

When her mother calls on the phone to ask how the plans are coming along, I feel foolish because I don't have much to tell her. I try to imagine her face through the line, round and strong, the braids in her hair, graying at the edge of her forehead. I only met her briefly at dinner a couple of months ago when she passed through Atlanta. I feel like I need to explain my love for her each and every time we speak, like I'm back in Dallas giving a presentation to a big group of bigwigs again, this time for someone important.

"I'll get Z for you," I say into the phone after a few niceties. I'd rehearsed each and every possible conversation with her, yet I am still never quite ready when I hear her voice on the other end of the phone.

"Let's get married at the Baptist church in Eton," she says one night while we're falling asleep to the *Tonight Show*. It seems smart; it was the same one Pa preached at, where her father's death had been mourned, where Pa was left to rest, where we'd first united on those stairs, where Ma prayed each week, where it seemed like most things began and ended in Eton, the center of it all. As a boy I could wander around the town, climb into trees, rest in dark alleys, roll in dirt, look out my bedroom window, and see that church steeple high above it all, in the distance, its arms crossed, waiting and watching. Somehow I always knew I'd make my way back to it because it was the only way to go, the only way I really knew.

"Yes, let's do it. It makes perfect sense, baby. Why not? Now go to sleep," I tell her, spooning her from behind.

Neither of us expected to end up back in Eton, it's true. There were so many reasons to go astray again: its heat and its dark dividing lines and the shadows of pasts that had created us, roots of pain, then sanguinity, the acidity of them both. But then there was its light, purple flowers on long green stems on the outskirts of town, the soft twist of the southern drawl of the locals, the mild temperatures and the dirt roads and the fresh air and the history, both the highs and the lows. It was our history. We'd thought of Myrtle Beach and the Bahamas or eloping in Vegas or traveling Europe, but we'd fallen in love with the idea of simplicity and the rest just faded into the background.

* * *

She stands before me in a simple white gown, strapless, and I am overcome by her, the curves of her shoulders, the swell of her stomach, the way two humans can come together and let everything between them fall to the ground. The ceremony is simple and quick; these walls have seen so much of my life, the rise and fall of it, birth and death and everything in between. We only invite a handful of people, our witnesses, and want the rest to ourselves.

Ma sits in the front row and she never takes her eyes off of us. I've never seen her look happier. She wears a long white dress, and her pantyhose make her look like she's just come from the beach. When the ceremony is over, she comes over and hugs us both at the same time.

"It was meant to be," she says. "Finally, something worked just like it was supposed to." She pulls her purse over her shoulder then and tells us she's going out for a smoke.

We can't wait to get back to our life together, waking up and going to sleep and eating and breathing, music on in the background, the stove always warm, our bellies full of laughter. It's what we've managed to create. We have money and we have choices and opportunities and places we want to go, but there was so much regular living that neither of us had ever done: we want it desperately.

After the ceremony, we eat a meal at the corner restaurant in town, an old antebellum mansion turned into something else, a big gathering place with linen tablecloths and the smell of catfish and peach cobbler, the glass chandeliers blowing in the wind so slightly, the open windows without screens and the lightning bugs entering the room and then leaving. To my right, my new wife; to my left, my mother. A new life growing; life was about to begin, and I can't remember anything else before this.

"To us, my love," she says, raising her pineapple juice.

"To us," I say, raising my glass higher, both of us swallowing the whole glass of juice.

*   *   *

I finally open that studio Pa always wanted; and soon for intrepid southerners, for whom tradition, comfort, and pride were foremost, the House of SinClair is the only way to go—comfy sofas covered in velvet, walnut consoles, and anything made of wood left au naturel, all carved and blessed by a hardworking man's hands, pieces that begin a heritage, befitting for parents to pass on to their children. Pa knew very little about bergères or marquises, yet many of his customers swore his pieces could be in any drawing room in Paris or Rome—rich hand-carved pieces with padded linen or leather upholstery, comfy sofas with floral fabrics, red velvet fabric chairs.

During my summers I worked alongside Pa, and I'd picked up more than I'd realized. Pa's tools called me daily.

Before he got sick, Pa was finishing a large order from the church, a dozen pieces, celebrant chairs, pulpit chairs, Christian crosses, high-back chairs, piano casters and credence tables. On the pastor's insistence, he had ordered heavenly red oak from up north. From the lumber to the kilns used in crafting the pieces, Pa took exceptional care to ensure everything was perfect. He worked on the pieces night and day; all there was left to do were the finishing touches.

I put the pieces in the showroom during the grand opening prior to shipping them off, along with other crisply carved pieces upholstered in satin and swish silk fabrics that Pa had named after Confederate generals; the Lee, the Stonewall, and the Mosby represented the virtues of southern nobility. Whether it was kitchen cupboard or sturdy mahogany tables for serving roasted pheasant or mantels for mounting wild boar and other game, Pa promised southern charm and delivered. There was so much more to that man than I realized.

In many ways, I had become him. I rose by five o'clock and worked till my body gave up. I was completely engrossed. Every now and then I'd be visited by Z in the workshop; I'd take a break, talk, laugh, caress my unborn, and go back to work.

There were days that we fell asleep on the old couch in my workshop watching the old fifties' TV. I'd place my head on Z's belly and feel our baby move over to where my hands were. I'd been praying for a son, and with the way Z's belly hung low, everyone swore my prayers had been answered.

*   *   *

"Life is funny, Carmine, ain't it?" Ma fills my cup up with coffee, and we sit together at the same old Formica table. I stare at the old knife lines in it, follow them as though I'm reading my own palm, predicting the future, seeing how and when and if one line will lead to another.

"I think life is simpler than we realize." I smile at her from across the table, reach for her hand.

"Yes, son, that's how it should be. I always used to tell your pa that, and I think he believed it in his own way. I think he just felt kinda like he needed to get things just so before they could be easy. Kinda backwards, don't you think?" She laughs, sits up straight. She's doing better than ever these days; she's got more life left in her than most. She's gained a little weight and cut her long hair short, and the kitchen smells like fried chicken again most days. She hangs laundry on the line. She even got herself a pair of new tennis shoes for taking walks at the park. I have never seen her this energetic.

"I never thought I'd get you back, Carmine; I thought I'd lost you forever. And now I got a grandbaby coming . . ." She puts her face in her hands and starts to cry softly. I get up from the table and hug her from behind.

"Yeah, it's like part two for us St. Clairs, isn't it? I think Pa would've liked sharing it with us."

"I know he would have. I know it."

*   *   *

Pastor Stanley walks into the room wearing a mustache and his same old broad smile.

"Haven't see you in a while, son. What's the occasion? Did someone die?" He laughs, pulls up a chair beside me.

"Not that I know of." I laugh and reach out to shake his hand. We sit down in our usual spots, as though no time has passed. He pours himself a cup of coffee from the pot on the table and pushes a cup toward me.

"I just wanted to tell you how much you've helped me, pastor. I mean, how you've helped me see how a person can cross the bridge between one big thing to another and get the whole picture."

"It's easier than you thought it would be, isn't it?" He crosses one leg over the other.

"I don't know why I fought it so long. The light, I mean. I don't know why I chose the path I did for so long. I mean, when I think about all the time I've wasted . . ."

"Stop there. Don't waste any of your time on that sort of thinking either, son. It doesn't pay. Not in any currency."

"I met this woman, this incredible woman, see? And we're going to have a baby . . ." I am talking so fast that I lose my breath.

"We're married now and my ma is better than I've ever seen her, and I realize how it all adds up to this now and I just want to feel worthy of it, you know, to trust it. I'm so worried that I'll mess up, that I'll mess this up."

"See? That's the thing right there. Where's your heart? What do you believe? If you only believe in the one thing— in the love, the life, the man you've become—you'll be okay. You don't believe in the other stuff anymore, right?"

I shake my head back and forth, look out the window and see the trees shake a few leaves off.

"Well, then, that's all that matters. Stay focused on the prize, Carmine, and you'll be all right. But remember that life has its own twists and turns, out of our control, and we have to go with them; we have to keep believing and creating and accepting." He smiles, drinks the last of his coffee, and stands up.

"I hate to cut our meeting short, but I've got some family business of my own to preserve. Come back and see me, though, whenever you'd like. Ya hear?"

I stand up and shake his hand, watch as he leaves the room, look out at the tree again. When I leave the room, I put my hand on my heart and smile.

CHAPTER 23

IT IS THREE IN the morning when the pains come, but her water doesn't break right away. I awake to her screaming, and for a fast second, I think it is Pa.

"Carmine, Carmine, something is happening, something has changed." She tells me this as she holds her stomach tightly, and when we stand up, we can see that he's dropped significantly and that he is ready, even if we are not.

"Just hold on, baby, just hold on. It's going to be okay." I turn on the bedroom light and throw on some clothes. She sits on the edge of the bed breathing heavily. I sit beside her and hold her hand.

"Where's your bag? Is it in the hall closet?"

She nods. Her face is so pale, I feel adrenaline pulse through my body.

I rush out of the room and look for her bag, turning on all the lights in the house in a panic. When I get back, she's laying on her side.

"Baby, what's wrong? What's wrong?" I remember scenes from movies, women in labor, the regularity of contractions; I can't place any of it now. Z's face is covered in sweat.

"It hurts so much, Carmine, so bad. Worse than anything I've ever felt, and something doesn't feel right . . . I don't know if . . ." She's crying so hard she loses her breath, begins to hyperventilate and scream.

That is the last that I remember, other than bits and pieces of ambulance lights and paramedics pushing into our bedroom, the big pool of blood on our baby blue sheets. The rest is a big red blur that stretches across my mind in vibrant circles that I try to catch with my hands because I think if I can catch them, I can change their shape, change history.

*   *   *

I am sitting in the waiting room with its pale walls and difficult furniture and lonely air when the doctor comes in to talk to me. He is older and gray, and his mustache stretches to the edge of his lips in black and gray; I am afraid of him in a way that fear has not shown me.

I know what he'll tell me. I was there, of course, for the biggest part of it. I watched her writhe and twist as Samuel tried to leave her body. I saw the beautiful brown leave her face in blotches, and I felt her grip loosen on my hand. The part that won't leave my mind is all the red, all the bleeding, all the crying, all the helplessness—and then the cries of my son as he left her womb. He didn't want to go.

I sit in that stale waiting room and I wait for him to tell me how we've lost her, and I want to scream how can that be because I had just found her and life couldn't possibly be that rotten and how am I supposed to raise a colored son with only white memories? I think about what Pastor Stanley's told me just a few days before, how I need to believe, keep my eye on the prize, and I want to scream.

"It's a rare bleeding disorder that we couldn't have known about before, son." He's talking and I hear the words, but they refuse to stick in my head; they're pounding on me, trying to get in. I feel as though I will explode.

"Your boy is healthy and strong, there's nothing you need to worry about there," he continues, and now he's sitting beside me on the pale sofa and his hand burns on my shoulder. I get up and walk around the small room. Overhead I hear people being paged on the intercom system.

"How could this have happened today? You could have done something, you should have done something!" I am screaming and my hands are on top of my head, and I am nearly running around the small room now in small, crazy circles.

"The problem is that her blood wouldn't clot and there was nothing . . ." I kick the small television stand in the corner and yell for him to shut up. He's telling me to calm down. I want to go back to the edge of our bed and hold her hand again and we'll rewrite it from there. Instead of driving to the hospital in Eton, we'll go to the big one in Atlanta and we'll pray; we'd forgotten to pray, and there, everything will be okay and we'll raise our son the way she wanted. And we'll teach him to honor both the light and dark within him, the way she'd taught me, and when we grow old together, our color will merge the way old paint does in a room of an old house.

I sit down and the doctor keeps watching me. In his eyes, there is pity, and it is looming and so sad that I have to look away.

"Where is she? Where is she right now?"

He tells me that she's still in her room, the one where she'd labored and delivered just moments before.

When I get back to the bright room, there is a curtain drawn around her bed and her hands have been folded on her empty stomach; there's a slight smile on her face, and I can't understand who put it there. She is a shade lighter, and the red of struggle has left her face. I fold both of her hands in mine, and they are still warm. Outside the day goes on as though nothing in the world has changed; I don't understand how the earth keeps on spinning.

It takes all my effort to keep breathing, in and out—I can't do it. I lay my head on her chest and beg her to come back. Z . . . my darling . . . baby, I can't do any of this without you. Baby, come back for me; we'll leave this world together, baby. I think I hear her heart beating beneath her skin, and I sit up straight and look at her. Her eyes are closed and she is so still, and I can't believe how something so big can pass so quietly.

The hours before come back to me, and I crawl over them inch by inch, looking for a reason, a way to change things, a clue. The labor pains were hard and they came fast and close together as we drove the few miles to the hospital. I'd even forgot to turn on the headlights, the night so dark, the cab of the truck so hot with our breathing.

"Carmine, make it stop; it hurts so much." She's holding her stomach, and I have her hand in mine and I drive as fast as the old truck will allow me.

I rush her into the front doors of the hospital, and I am nearly carrying her. "Make it stop hurting," I yell through the hallways. "Give her something now; she's hurting too much. Now, people, now!" The urgency reminds me of sailors on sinking ships, trying to ward off their fate and the water and the fear of their fellow men.

Once we are settled into her room, we are both calmer, but the medicine is not working and the labor is coming faster than expected and our baby is inching down the birth canal. The screams begin when the pills wear off, and they tell us it's too late for an epidural and that she'll have to continue natural because he's coming too fast. She screams into the early morning hours, and I cry and I sweat but I never stop holding her. And then the doctors realize she's bleeding too much and that her body isn't stopping it and our baby is almost here but she is growing weaker.

By the time they use the big metal forceps to pull him from her, she has lost consciousness and the room is so eerily quiet before his cries come. There is life. When I look at him, I see Z's black hair in large curls all over his head. They take him away, she stops breathing, and they make me leave the room.

*   *   *

I remember life in fragments after that: the way her hand gradually went from warm to cold, the way I gripped it in an effort to keep her from going to the other side, and finally, the way my baby boy looked from the outside of the nursery glass. He is swollen, tender, already so full of his mother's light, his skin the faintest of browns, his eyes wide-open while all the other babies cry with closed eyes. I watch him from the glass for hours, don't take him when the nurses offer him bundled to me, cry when I think about going home alone. Ma came up to the hospital after Z had been gone for hours. I don't know who called her, but someone did.

"Carmine, show me your son. She's gone, I know, but your son is here. He's here and waiting." I take her to the edge of the nursery glass, to my post, and I watch as the nurses feed him and change him and place a soft blue hat on his round head. I won't let Ma go in to him. I don't want to jar anything out of place, make it permanent; if I hold still long enough, things can go back to the way they were.

*   *   *

When midnight comes and Samuel enters his second day of life, Z's second day of death, I go back to her room and stare out the window at the moon. My son has been alive twelve hours, and I haven't put him in my arms or allowed my mother to do so. I am so afraid the St. Clairs will curse him, ruin him with our touch.

I leave the hospital the next morning and go back to our small, country house. When I come through the front door, I fall to my knees: she is there, I can feel it. The house smells of her, contains her, contains us; and without her, I know it is on its way to decay. I cry into my hands as I walk from room to room, taking her all in: the nursery she'd prepared in blues and yellows, the books that line the hallway: African literature and Victorian novels and long hardbacks of poetry and sonnets and songs she'd sing to me in the night.

For the first few minutes, it is easy for me to forget about our baby boy, to forget that my beloved is laying in a dark, cold room in the basement of the hospital, to not realize anything has changed at all. The sun still reaches into the tall windows of our house and stretches across the sofa and the hardwood floors; the coffee, set to brew the night before, is cold in its full carafe; snapshots are still in magnets on the refrigerator. Nothing has changed at all. Z would be coming back in from her walk any moment now that she'd quit jogging, and she'd bring fruit from the old man's stand: pineapple and mangos and avocados for lunch, and all of this would let me forget that the past I'd lived didn't matter at all now that I had a future with her.

My son's face comes back to me as I caress her dress that is stretched across the bed in a patch of sunlight. My baby's skin, the very perfect nuance of color, the big round circles so perfectly formed in his hair, the puffiness of my nose on his face, her chin, the almond of her eyes, my forehead, and the creation that couldn't have been completed without us. I want to hold him, to love him, but I don't know that it's possible without her; I don't know that life can go forward without her, without her love, without Pa to hate, without something to have and to hold, to cherish or despise.

I leave the house and start walking until I get to Main Street. I find a café next to the old bank building and go in and sit down. I order a grilled cheese and watch people as they pass the large window in front. The world looks so very different to me, all of it, the lines and the morphing, even the way my sandwich, the bread and the cheese, are melted together; everything is suddenly so separate and so isolated. I feel alone, so alone, so heavy, and I try to forget my boy for just a few moments at a time because seeing him, realizing him, is knowing that she is gone, and I refuse to accept it.

I eat the sandwich and drink the cold coffee and get up again to walk the streets, to notice people's colors and habits and clothing and how many of them might be dead tomorrow. I want to stop to yell this in their faces: "Don't get too comfortable, people," I'd say, "it could all be fucking gone before you know it." My pace quickens as I think of the confrontation and how resistance comes so easily to me. I walk and walk, past the railroad tracks again, past the restaurant where we ate dinner on our wedding night, and then suddenly I stop walking and look to the sky because I'm so tired and feel as though I don't know how my legs work anymore or how my heart will continue to pump blood or how my hands will feed my mouth or how I'll ever be able to see anything again.

I can't walk hard or long enough. I can't get away from what is true, no matter how hard I try. I beg the sky for relief: God, I can't do it. I just can't do it. I'm not that man.

*   *   *

When I walk into Ma's house, she is on the sofa smoking; the smell of the menthol air is comforting to me, and I take two big lungfuls of it before sitting down on my end of the couch. I can feel her looking at me, but I don't speak. I don't think I remember how to form words, and I don't even know if there are really thoughts occupying spaces in my head.

"Where's your baby, son?" One of her legs rests over the other, and her foot bounces and she takes long drags off her cigarette, the inhale and the exhale, two separate things.

"He's not my baby, Ma; he was hers. I don't think I can do it." Ma comes up beside me. I want Z back.

"You got to let all of that go, boy. Life isn't fair, honey, and there's nothing I can say to you about that." She's rubbing the small of my back, and I can never remember her doing that. I am her baby again; I don't want to be a man or a father or a widow, and I don't want to move.

She brings me a glass of water and a wet rag, which she places on the back of my neck, and it feels so good and so soothing that I put my hand on top of it and push on my neck to feel the coolness even deeper. I lean back on the sofa and blink a few times to clear my eyes, to push the rest of the tears down my face.

"I'm serious, Ma. I don't know how to be a father. I would hate to fail him. I am nothing without her; I don't have anything to offer him without her to hold me up. See what I'm saying, Ma?" The feeling is starting to come back to my skin, and I look around at the clean house and how the drapes are wide-open and this room, once so dark, is so alive and my mom's dress is yellow and not brown.

"Carmine, you have your own light. You always did. For a long while, your pa and I shaded you with our own darkness, and then you did a good job of it yourself, but you have your own light. You do. It's the only light your son needs to grow. We've got to get that baby home. You've got to take him to his home, and you've got to be his father." She's rocking on the sofa a little, remembering something.

"You know son, life is nothing more than a series of choices. If you want to do right by that baby, by your son, you do one right thing at a time. You start by bringing him home, and the stuff you don't know about him and how to take care of him, you learn, and you get up each day and you start over. You do one right thing at a time, boy, and it'll be all right."

CHAPTER 24

Z HAS SOME FAMILY in South Carolina that I need to call. I've been sitting in our bedroom for hours now, maybe days, the phone ringing off the hook, the hospital's number popping up, my cell phone ringing with calls from Ma. I feel paralyzed, want to hold the pause button forever, wonder what would happen if I stay like this, in place.

I hear a knock on the door, stop breathing for a second, imagine that it's the police coming to get me, to finally punish me for all my wrongs, to tell me time has caught up with me, that all of this is really true.

I sit there and the knocking gets louder, becomes a pounding. I stretch my legs and then get up. I hear ringing in my ears, hear the hum of the refrigerator; outside, Z's wind chimes settle.

When I open the door, a small man stands there, wearing a casual suit, looking straight at me. Behind him, I see the trash truck pass, the mailman across the street, life goes on. How could it?

"Are you Carmine St. Clair?" His face is warm, his eyes tender; he reaches out his hand to shake mine.

"I am," I say quietly. I feel a chill slide up my spine and then back.

"I'm from Eton Social Services. The hospital has called me because you've not held your son or made arrangements to pick him up. Is that true?" He's holding a folder in his hand, a manila rectangular; a few yellow papers stick out.

I look at him, don't recognize him, can barely understand the words that escape his mouth.

"Listen, Mr. St. Clair. I know your wife passed in childbirth and you must be in a real state of shock, but we've got to make some arrangements here . . ."

"I need to sit down for a minute. I just need a minute here. Do you want to come in?" I turn around and walk toward the sofa, hear his quiet footsteps behind me.

I sit on the soft and he sits on the other end, hands me his card.

"As I was saying, your son is healthy, and the hospital normally only holds newborns twenty-four hours. It's been three days now, and I need to know what your plans are."

"Did you ever go to a movie, get up to use the bathroom, get popcorn or a drink, and when you came back, you were lost? I mean, you miss one part, one key scene, and lose your grasp on the story? I mean never catch up. So when the end of the movie comes along, you aren't really sure what happened? I mean, you don't understand how what you missed changed everything you thought you knew.

"I used to go to matinees in Dallas all the time—that's where I used to live—and this seemed to happen to me all the time. I'd step away for just a few minutes—to make a phone call or take a piss—and that was all it took for me to lose it, I mean the story. I'd come out of the theater confused, feel ripped off. I mean, how can you miss one thing and lose it all? That's how I feel now. How did I get here? From there? From bliss? It doesn't make any sense."

He looks at me for a long time, like a child, searching my face for some kind of clue.

"I think I know what you mean, sir, I think so. Life is funny like that; it doesn't always make sense, the why or the what. But the fact remains that I need to know . . ."

"I need to know, too. I need to know what I am supposed to do with a baby boy and a dead wife? What do you tell people in situations like this?" I rub my hands on the legs of my jeans until they are warm and I am sweating behind my ears.

"I tell them that they've got to keep moving forward, that they can't stop, that they need to focus on what means the most to them and do everything in their power. I need to know that you'll do that, Carmine. I need to know that you're going to pick up your baby and take good care of him. And if you're not going to—well, I need to know that too. That's why I'm here. What are you going to do?"

*   *   *

I get up and go to the small telephone table in the hallway. I find the address book with names and numbers of cousins and other relatives Z invited to the wedding. I don't know these people much, and I have to tell them that they've lost a family member and gained one, too. All in the same breath.

I start with A and call Aunt Marla first. When she answers, I can't speak at first.

"Hello? Hello?" Her voice searches the line.

"Marla. I mean, Aunt Marla. Hello, this is Carmine, Carmine St. Clair. I'm Z's husband. I'm calling to tell you . . ."

"Yes, I remember you. Where's Z? What's wrong? I've been calling her for days now. Did she have the baby?"

241

"She did, she did, and the baby is fine. He's fine, he's good, but Z, Z . . ." I choke on my words, try to spit them out, push them out of my mouth.

"Speak up. What is it?" She's yelling into the phone, and I can hear her mouth push against the receiver.

I take a deep breath, try to finish, to complete the one sentence I've never spoken aloud.

"Marla, oh god, Marla, I mean Aunt Marla, Z . . . she started to bleed really bad, I mean, she started to bleed at home and things went so fast and . . ."

"Spit it out, boy!" She's screaming into the phone now.

"I don't know what to do. I don't . . ."

"Tell me what's wrong with my niece right now, or I will . . ."

"She's dead, Marla, she's dead. She bled to death on the table while she delivered our son." I yell it at her, get it out of me as fast as I can.

"You're lying, you're lying to me. Z was so healthy and strong and . . ." I hear her sobbing now, a heavy, bulky kind of cry. It scares me.

"It's true. It's true. She's no longer with us."

"What did you do to her? How did this happen?" She's taking short breaths on the other end of the line, hyperventilating. I pace the room and sweat.

"The doctors said there was nothing they could do . . . that the bleeding disorder is rare and we couldn't have known . . ."

"I don't believe that. I don't believe that. You. If she'd never gotten involved with some hick white man . . ."

My legs fold beneath me and I fall to the floor. "Don't say that . . . don't say that!"

I hang up the phone and ask Ma to call every third person on the list.

*   *   *

I leave the house just as the afternoon sun is starting to tuck behind the clouds and retire. I walk, but slowly this time, and I make the right turn and the next thing I know, I'm standing at the nursery window again, watching my son twist and turn in his white sleeper, his fists clenched, his eyes bright, not an ounce of fear in them. I remember that her body is floors beneath us, but I also know that can't be true of her spirit. "I'm always with you, baby, my love; it's the only way it can be," she'd always tell me as she explained that she'd felt we'd always been together, that it just took us awhile to realize that, to come home, and that it just wasn't possible to leave that state ever. I pull the collar of my shirt up and I smell her so strongly in the fibers that I rest my head on my own shoulder while I watch him. He is so calm and so strong already, but I can't bring myself to go in there, to stand before him just yet.

I leave the hospital and the sky turns gray as I walk home, and then to black. When I get inside the door, I don't turn on any lights or use the bathroom or breathe a lot, but just climb inside our bed, clothes and all, and wrap myself tightly in our sheets. My sleep is a big black envelope that blocks me from the world, from the truth.

When I wake up in the morning, I step into a cold shower and stand still until my body adjusts to the harsh temperature. I stay under the water until my skin takes on a bluish tone and I've run the soap all over my face and my neck and I've cried and I've sat on the bottom of the tub like a child. When I step out, the same heaviness is on me, the same ugly truths, but I'm ready to put on a clean shirt and to tie my shoes one at a time and go to him. To stand up. I have failed at so much in my life, but I can't fail at this. I cannot run from him.

I load his car seat and I start the car and let it idle in the drive awhile. I try to remember ever holding a baby, ever—I don't think I have. I've seen them in grocery stores and in church pews and on TV, but there has never been a single time that I've held one or looked into its small eyes. When

Z was pregnant, I tried to imagine everything about my baby's face: every fold of his skin and every newly formed reflex and the slate of his clean mind. When he began to kick in her womb, I placed my hand near the kick each and every time, taking him all in, letting my love for him, for her, consume me and melt every defense. I wanted to learn him, to study him, to understand the cycle of life, the human body, the essence of God. I'd just never imagined that I'd have to do it alone.

Instead of driving straight to the hospital, I stop at a bookstore and buy every baby and parenting book I can find: *The Baby Whisperer* and *Doctor Spock* and others. Z had grown up with babies, had many nieces and nephews, promised to teach me all I would need to know. I'd planned to follow her lead, to learn by the unfolding of each day. Advertising and martini lunches and salesmanship cannot help me now.

I grow excited as I drive, then angry, then panic takes over. What is this new world? What is this life? I remember Mom telling me about doing one right thing at a time. I feel Z's voice vibrate in my mind, know she is there in some way. She has to be.

When I get to the hospital, I am out of breath. I've spent the last few miles of the drive imagining my boy at various ages: a teenager, a wobbly toddler, an awkward boy of ten. An infant. I am alone.

I park the car and sit in the driver's seat and watch a couple leaving the hospital. The father. I watch him. I notice his movements. His hand on the small of his wife's back, his hand firmly on the handle of the baby's carrier. He sets the baby down by the car, pulls the blanket back from its face, smiles; he pulls from something way down deep. I watch as he leans into the backseat to buckle him into the car seat, how he closes the door gently, picks up the bag, and leads his tired wife to the passenger side, how he looks off into the horizon before getting in the car himself. I want to follow him home. I want to see how it's done. I want to know it can be as easy as they make it look.

I walk, nearly run, into the hospital, skipping up six flights of stairs when the elevator takes too long. I can feel something take over. I am no longer myself, the man I know; someone else has come to take his place. It's a strange, hollow feeling, almost euphoric; I've got to move, I've got to chase it because I can't lose.

"I'm ready to take my son home. I want to take my son home." I repeat myself at the first face I see at the nurse's station. I don't wait for an answer but run to the nursery glass to set my eyes on him. His bed is empty; adrenaline takes over.

"I want my baby! Where is my goddamn baby?" I am pacing the halls and looking at each uniformed face, demanding to know where he is; everything has hit me at once—I can't lose him too. I'll never let him go, never walk away from him again. I start to run back to the nurse's station, and they tell me to lower my voice, that my baby is fine, but I can't calm myself; I need him in my arms now. When I pause to take a breath, I see a yellow-haired nurse coming up behind me pushing a small bed on wheels. Samuel is in it. My arms drop to my side.

"Carmine, here is your son. He was being bathed. He's been waiting for you awhile now." She smiles and pushes the car toward me. I am standing in the middle of the hallway with my son and my wife is dead and the room begins to spin, so I push the bed to a nearby chair. I sit down and pull him close to me. His eyes are wide, and before I can stop it, he looks right at me. His eyes lock with mine, and I feel something come over me that is at first very frightening, and then calming and soothing, I know in that very instant: I am no longer who I was.

When I take him into my arms, soft skin and all, we both let out a whimper, and I breathe so shallowly and take his small parts into my lungs and put his head and small body against my chest, on my shoulder, and I feel her: she is with us. I lean back in my chair and cry and laugh at the same time, and both hurt.

CHAPTER 25

WITHOUT THE LIGHT BEHIND her skin, Z's brown skin looks dull and flat, like the pasty brown used in preschool projects and Spanish architecture. I hate this. I walk around the funeral home with an unsettling energy in my feet, pushing my shoes forward, my son on my shoulder; I've not left him or been more than a foot away from him since picking him up from the hospital. He breathes so softly under my chin; it is poetry, the sound of his living. His skin is so delicate and pink and light brown, the smell of him greater than anything I've ever gotten close to; there is something so big about him.

I cannot sit still even long enough to answer the funeral director's questions about the service and about who will speak and for how long and where the flowers should be placed or how many people will ride in the town car to the grave site. I just want him to quit talking. I want to walk out of the old and aging building and back home to my house, our house, and pretend that she will walk in the door at any moment. I just want to pretend a little longer.

"Make it as simple and as beautiful and as quick as possible. That's what I want. Make that happen."

He looks back at me, smiles quietly; his eyes blink a few times and he nods. He's a small man, probably fell into this work, a family's business maybe; his heart's not in it. I feel sorry for him, but he's good at this job, riding out people's waves of emotion. I can be hard; I try to be easy on him.

"I don't much care about this part, but others will. Don't let it stretch on too long—it hurts too much—but don't rush it either. Play the calypso music I gave you at the end, run the slide show, usher us through it. Show us how it's done. Can you do that?"

"Of course, sir, of course. Don't worry about a thing." When I turn to leave, I think I see him wink at me out of the corner of his eye, his soft brown eye peeking from his thick lid. I wince. He doesn't know me like that.

Z's family is sitting down in the main room, and their faces make all of this hard; the resemblance is so strong, especially in the eyes, and you cannot not look at someone's eyes when you speak to them. They want to hold my baby, and the thought of the cold spot on my chest scares me; without my son, I'm afraid I'll run down the street like a crazy, grieving husband, and then maybe they'll take my baby from me.

I try to smile when I see my old friends sitting behind me wearing T-shirts and jeans, Griff looking solemn yet still jolly, Mark's eyes red, his foot tapping, both with a mouth full of tobacco. My mother sits in the last row, empty chairs on each side of her; there are no other St. Clairs to help us grieve this loss, to help fill our rows and the big, looming space left by this and the other. We make eye contact and she smiles back at me, big but not happy. I remember how I used to look at her from the school bus window and feel comforted by her face. There she is again. I barely recognize the woman she has become since Pa's death. Kindness, tenderness, love—it all seems to come so easily to her now that she's free. I wonder if this is who she was all along, buried beneath the weight of Pa.

Busloads of Z's friends and family come out. A couple of Z's cousins stand up and talk about spending summers with her, about her laugh and her playfulness and her genuine kindness and her enduring spirit; and when they are done, everyone looks to me. Part of me believes that anything I would say would take away from her, her life, what she meant, what she means. I find strength in my legs and walk up to the podium. My baby stirs.

"I . . . I just want to say that I didn't know life could be so good, so sweet. She taught me that. To just relax and to enjoy life and love the right way and . . . I'm so afraid I'll forget, that somehow I'll lose . . ." I start to choke, feel my knees grow weak beneath me, take a breath and hold it.

"Thank you all for coming." I stand there for a few minutes looking at everyone, pat my baby's back as I take my seat. Pastor Stanley comes and takes my place and says some words from the Bible about death not really being death at all. I let out a big audible sigh because I don't know if it's true. I look around at others' faces to see if it makes a difference for them. To see if they believe that once someone is there, they're always there. This I want to believe. Z's family comes to me, one by one, leaning into my neck for hugs, patting the baby's back, crying big messy tears.

"Carmine, love that baby the best you can."

"Carmine, she loved you, she loved you so much. She talked about you constantly."

"Carmine, be strong, pray, you ain't never really alone."

"Carmine, I'm sorry. Real sorry. Z was a great woman and . . ."

I stop listening after awhile, gaze off somewhere, blink my eyes and lean into people as they come close, but I've already escaped.

I stay in the big empty room for a long time after everyone shuffles out to the lobby for coffee, small sandwiches—what do all the rituals really mean?

I ask that the coffin be left open, that I be the one to close her in the darkness, that I be the last one to see her darling face.

I see Ma at the doorway heading out. She looks at me for a long time. I wave her off softly, hold her gaze for a few seconds; she understands, closes the door behind her.

I put Samuel down in his seat, slide a blanket up to his chin. When I walk up to the coffin, my eyes play tricks; it looks like her eyes are open and she's looking at me.

I step back a few feet, look at her closer; she's there but not, her eyes closed completely.

I reach for her hand; it feels cold, so cold. I want to jerk my hand away but I don't. I want this.

"Baby . . . why did you have to go? Why did you have to go?" I squeeze her hand so tightly, fold my fingers into hers.

"Come back, baby, please come back . . ." I cry so hard I choke on my own tears, but then the baby stirs, his tiny hands form fists, and I stop.

"I don't know if I can do this, Z. We were supposed to do this . . . I need you so much. Who am I without you?"

Her face seems to change expressions, like some hologram of memories, her laughing, her angry that I'd left the empty milk carton in the fridge, her cheeks full in the last month of pregnancy.

I stand there for a long time, wait for her to respond. Outside I can hear car doors slam, hushed voices making plans.

"Z . . . this can't be it. What am I supposed to do here? I can't put you into the ground. You don't belong in the ground . . ." My sobs have grown violent and loud. I look up at the ceiling and want to scream.

Samuel stirs again. His head moves back and forth; he's dreaming but awake. Suddenly his eyes open, search the sky for something, and he starts to cry.

I run to him, take him out of his seat, fold him into my arms and walk back to the casket.

"Z . . . look at him, look at you in him. You never even got to see him." I turn the baby's face toward hers for just a second, pull him closer.

I feel the funeral director's stares coming from the back of the room; life keeps on moving. Time can be so pushy and so demanding, and I wonder why we can't just stop it for a while.

"Mr. St. Clair. The town car is waiting outside whenever you are ready. Your mom will ride with you, and of course, myself. Take your time." His voice is as black as the suit he's wearing, and I wonder how he can do this job day after day and how he's able to separate his own life from all of this death. I believe it's possible that he can only achieve a sorta gray existence, with death at each of his corners.

"All right. I'll be there in a few minutes." I don't take my eyes off of Z as I say it.

"I've got to let you go now, baby. I've got to keep on moving; I've got to somehow accept this." I lean down and kiss her forehead; it is not hers anymore. I fold her hands over her heart, close the lid as slow as I can.

After a few minutes, I stand up and grab Samuel's bag and head to the men's room to change him.

"Baby boy, my son, my child. There's something we've got to go and do right now, and it's gonna be hard. It makes me so sorry that you have to start your life already burdened by this, but I've learned something important that I'm going to teach you. There are just some things you simply have to accept because the only alternative is spending your life fighting with them. Your mother is the most beautiful person I've ever known, and now we have to go watch as her body is laid into the ground to rest. It doesn't make any sense but we'll do it together, and it'll be okay." I sigh deep into my chest to hold back the tears as I button his sleeper back up and lift him from the changing table. I've got to give him all I have.

The grave site is cold and the wind gusts as if in defiance; even the sun tries to cower behind the clouds before they move across the sky. There is no way around this part. There are only a couple of rows of black chairs set up in front of the prepared ground. Z's family hold their faces and Ma keeps her head down, but I watch Z's casket because I feel like I've got to keep her safe, even now, and when the preacher begins to speak again about the shadow and the valley of death and about ashes we come and ashes we leave, that is when I begin to cry and hold my son and beg for the strength to mold his life on my own. Beneath the tears, anger tries to boil to the surface, but I no longer have the soil within myself to grow it, and I let it subside and surrender to the pain, softly and quietly, to the love beneath my hands, the warmth of my baby son, the way it is and will be.

The funeral car leaves the grave site when the men have shoveled dirt upon my beloved's wood box and the flowers have been removed and the tractor to move the earth on top of her has been gassed. The family has gone back to their hotels, and I promise to visit them before they go and apologize again for not having anything further back at the house—food, music, picture collages, a celebration of

Z's life. All of that seems ridiculous to me—the whole idea of celebrating someone's life after it has been jerked away from them. To me, it is like celebrating someone's days of walking after they've been paralyzed by an accident and their legs no longer work.

When the car drops me off and I tell Ma good-bye in the backseat of it, my bones feel heavy and achy from the day, and even the small task of unbuckling Samuel's car seat seems laborious and emotional. Z is immediate when I walk through the threshold of our front door: the sweet smell of her lilac skin is embedded in the walls, and when I walk through the living room to the kitchen, I can see her dancing in front of the stereo in cutoffs and praising the sounds of the calypso music while I laugh and shake my head.

I catch a glimpse of my face in the silver refrigerator, and my skin looks pasty and old but I don't dwell and instead start making bottles, enough to get us through the night, and I walk back into Samuel's room; the mobile still plays above him while he sleeps. I sit on the floor beside his crib and stay there until I hear him stir again.

*   *   *

When I go to sleep now, I think about Z, and sometimes I get an erection, but not the same kind. Sometimes with the pleasure of orgasm, I want to scream out in that way again. But without her praise, it means nothing. I get hard like flowers must rise for the sun; at the thought of her, I am longing, yearning, searching, wanting, needing to grow. Beside me, the bed is always empty, and I am still just me, still a man who dreams of leaving this body and flying above the clouds in search of her.

But I go on.

*   *   *

There are no individual days after that. Only memories that take me out of the present. Only fits of grief and moments of weakness, where I don't quite know if my body will lead me, hold me, so I can do what I have to do.

In the morning, I get up an hour early just so I can watch him sleep. In the day, I can't see a thing; he's a blur of action, emotion, reaching and pulling with every breath. In that hour just before he wakes up, I am one with her, with us, and these thoughts get me through the day.

It has only been three years since that night at that musty bar. I feel a million years older, mummified, strangled, and hung up to dry, but it has only been three years. Time really does nothing for life, adds nothing to the sum of existence. It only forces us to package events, feelings, things that weren't meant to have such parameters. But without time, everything becomes a breeding ground for hopelessness.

Time has never done me any favors this way, but we still live hand in hand.

I think back to that night in her car, mornings watching her sleep, feeling the curve of her breast beneath a dress I'll always look for in the windows of shops that I pass by.

I get to the shop by nine every morning, but before I get there, I see the wood chips on the floor and smell the sum of my life in short bursts of air that rush in the car window. I live for these things now. All of my senses are alive.

The drive to work is short and familiar, and I take the same route every day because it soothes me. There is still the pull of the drink and the drunk, the whore and the fuck, and I know it will live inside of me forever. I have found prayer to be a useful substitute these days. I've found baptism and the church on the poor side of town. On Sunday mornings, I put on one of those old suits and I pray. On my knees, I pray. And when I pray, I cry. And when I cry, big wet tears drop to the floor, and then I'm gone. Before the sermon is over, before the niceties can be exchanged, before the donuts are served, I am gone; and for a week, I am better, able to go on and live and be the thing I need to be. It is still only in front of God that I can release those tears. But this time, I cry another river, another tale, another story completely.

On Mondays, the day after those Sundays, I drive to work and see Eton for the first time. It is drab, I know; it is a useless corner of the earth, I know that, too, but it is ground and dirt and it speaks a million memories, like every other plot of land. And for now, I stay.